Two Novels by Nathanael West

N. Wallenstein Weinstein

1903 - 1940

Two Novels by

Noonday Press
a division of
Farrar, Straus and Company : New York

NATHANAEL WEST

The Dream Life of Balso Snell

A Cool Million

1931

The Dream Life of Balso Snell

Not the best of his books -- but
most available, & gives a
very simple & clear picture
of West. Became immediately
famous at his death. Married
the gal Eileen about whom
"My Sister Eileen" was written
This made him famous.
___

A fine example of a
"tendency" in Am. fiction
during the 30's.
(Indicate) Travesty of saints' lives.
Dostoevsky, Beaudelaire.
Puts himself in the Surrealist School
everything is ash -- emphereyed yach
experience - art is form - new forms →

e.g. observation of dreams.
"People are children locked
inside aging bodies -- longing
to mature, but unable to.
<u>Dream Life</u> -- incorporates this
the book has nothing to do with
anything in reality

"Dream" Books - Usually allegorical
                   Deals with mystery
                              (God)
1. Pilgrim's Progress
2. Gulliver's Travels

3. Aeneid
4. Piers Plowman
5. the Pearl
        Those that deal with spiritual
        truths are allegorical

        Freudian symbols are not
        allegorical because of being
        heavily rationalistic

According to Freud:
Allegorical thought - an evasion --
1. creates ideal world
2. Posits perfection which cannot be
   reached.
3. creates a reality which is not
   there (reality is within you)

St. Puce – transcended his role as flea –– becomes "holy" flea. In reality he becomes so egotistical that he does not really transcend, but becomes blown-up with self-love.

Circularity – cycle of self-love

Acceptance & rejection (undercutting) occurs repeatedly.

West assumes that his audience is interested in avant-garde literature --- especially true of _Dream Life_. Not true of _Miss Lonely Hearts_, which is rooted in his own experience. Great deal of symbolic material in the book. This is atypical of the surrealist school.

To A. S.

"After all, my dear fellow,
life, Anaxagoras has said,
is a journey."
BERGOTTE

1

While walking in the tall grass that has sprung up around the city of Troy, Balso Snell came upon the famous wooden horse of the Greeks. A poet, he remembered Homer's ancient song and decided to find a way in.

On examining the horse, Balso found that there were but three openings: the mouth, the navel, and the posterior opening of the alimentary canal. The mouth was beyond his reach, the navel proved a cul-de-sac, and so, forgetting his dignity, he approached the last. O Anus Mirabilis!

Symbol of Projection

Along the lips of the mystic portal he discovered writings which after a little study he was able to decipher. Engraved in a heart pierced by an arrow and surmounted by the initial N, he read, "Ah! Qualis . . . Artifex . . . Pereo!" Not to be outdone by the actor-emperor, Balso carved with his penknife another heart and the words "O Byss! O Abyss! O Anon! O Anan!" omitting, however, the arrow and his initial.

Before entering he prayed:

"O Beer! O Meyerbeer! O Bach! O Offenbach! Stand me now as ever in good stead."

Balso immediately felt like the One at the Bridge, the Two in the Bed, the Three in the Boat, the Four on Horseback, the Seven Against Thebes. And with a high heart he entered the gloom of the foyer-like lower intestine.

After a little while, seeing no one and hearing nothing, Balso began to feel depressed. To keep his heart high and yet out of his throat, he made a song.

Round as the Anus
Of a Bronze Horse
Or the Tender Buttons
Used by Horses for Ani

On the Wheels of His Car
Ringed Round with Brass
Clamour the Seraphim
Tongues of Our Lord

Full Ringing Round
As the Belly of Silenus
Giotto Painter of Perfect Circles
Goes . . . One Motion Round

Round and Full
Round and Full as

A Brimming Goblet
The Dew-Loaded Navel
Of Mary
Of Mary Our Mother

Round and Ringing Full
As the Mouth of a Brimming Goblet
The Rust-Laden Holes
In Our Lord's Feet.
Entertain the Jew-Driven Nails.

He later gave this song various names, the most successful of which were: *Anywhere Out of the World, or a Voy-*
age Through the Hole in the Mundane Millstone and *At*
Hoops with the Ani of Bronze Horses, or Toe Holes for a
Flight of Fancy.

But despite the gaiety of his song, Balso did not feel sure
of himself. He thought of the Phoenix Excrementi, a race of
men he had invented one Sunday afternoon while in bed,
and trembled, thinking he might well meet one in this
place. And he had good cause to tremble, for the Phoenix
Excrementi eat themselves, digest themselves, and give
birth to themselves by evacuating their bowels.

Hoping to attract the attention of an inhabitant, Balso
shouted as though overwhelmed by the magnificence of his
surroundings:

"O the Rose Gate! O the Moist Garden! O Well! O Fountain! O Sticky Flower! O Mucous Membrane!"

A man with "Tours" embroidered on his cap stalked out
of the shadow. In order to prove a poet's right to trespass,
Balso quoted from his own works:

"If you desire to have two parallel lines meet at once or
even in the near future," he said, "it is important to make
all the necessary arrangements beforehand, preferably by
wireless."

The man ignored his little speech. "Sir," he said, "you are

an ambassador from that ingenious people, the inventors and perfectors of the automatic water-closet, to my people who are the heirs of Greece and Rome. As your own poet has so well put it, 'The Grandeur that was Greece and the Glory that was Rome' . . . I offer you my services as guide. First you will please look to the right where you will see a beautiful Doric prostate gland swollen with gladness and an over-abundance of good cheer."

This speech made Balso very angry. "Inventors of the automatic water-closet, are we?" he shouted. "Oh, you stinker! Doric, bah! It's Baptist '68, that's what it is. And no prostate gland either, simply an atrophied pile. You call this dump grand and glorious, do you? Have you ever seen the Grand Central Station, or the Yale Bowl, or the Holland Tunnel, or the New Madison Square Garden? Exposed plumbing, stinker, that's all I see—and at this late date. It's criminally backward, do you hear me?"

The guide gave ground before Balso's rage. "Please sir," he said, "please . . . After all, the ages have sanctified this ground, great men have hallowed it. In Rome do as the Romans do."

"Stinker," Balso repeated, but less ferociously this time.

The guide took heart. "Mind your manners, foreigner. If you don't like it here, why don't you go back where you came from? But before you go let me tell you a story—an old tale of my people, rich in local color. And, you force me to say it, apropos, timely. However, let me assure you that I mean no offense. The title of the story is

"VISITORS

"A traveler in Tyana, who was looking for the sage Appolonius, saw a snake enter the lower part of a man's body. Approaching the man, he said:

"'Pardon me, my good fellow, but a snake just entered your . . .' He finished by pointing.

"'Yes sir, he lives there,' was the astounding rejoinder.

"'Ah, then you must be the man I'm looking for, the philosopher-saint, Appolonius of Tyana. Here is a letter of introduction from my brother George. May I see the snake please? Now the opening. Perfect!'"

Balso echoed the last word of the story. "Perfect! Perfect! A real old-world fable. You may consider yourself hired."

"I have other stories to tell," the guide said, "and I shall tell them as we go along. By the way, have you heard the one about Moses and the Burning Bush? How the prophet rebuked the Bush for speaking by quoting the proverb, 'Good wine needs no bush'; and how the Bush insolently replied, 'A hand in the Bush is worth two in the pocket.'"

Balso did not consider this story nearly as good as the other; in fact he thought it very bad, yet he was determined to make no more breaks and entered the large intestine on the arm of his guide. He let the guide do all the talking and they made great headway up the tube. But, unfortunately, coming suddenly upon a place where the intestine had burst through the stomach wall, Balso cried out in amazement:

"What a hernia! What a hernia!"

The guide began to splutter with rage and Balso tried to pacify him by making believe he had not meant the scenery. "Hernia," he said, rolling the word on his tongue. "What a pity childish associations cling to beautiful words such as hernia, making their use as names impossible. Hernia! What a beautiful name for a girl! Hernia Hornstein! Paresis Pearlberg! Paranoia Puntz! How much more pleasing to the ear [and what other sense should a name please?] than Faith Rabinowitz or Hope Hilkowitz."

But Balso had only blundered again. "Sirrah!" the guide cried in an enormous voice, "I am a Jew! and whenever anything Jewish is mentioned, I find it necessary to say that I am a Jew. I'm a Jew! A Jew!"

"Oh, you mistake me," Balso said, "I have nothing against the Jews. I admire the Jews; they are a thrifty race. Some of my best friends are Jews." But his protests availed him little until he thought to quote C. M. Doughty's epigram. "The semites," Balso said with great firmness, "are like to a man sitting in a cloaca to the eyes, and whose brows touch heaven."

When Balso had at last succeeded in quieting the guide, he tried to please him further by saying that the magnificent tunnel stirred him to the quick and that he would be satisfied to spend his remaining days in it with but a few pipes and a book.

The guide tossed up his arms in one of those eloquent gestures the latins know so well how to perform and said: "After all, what is art? I agree with George Moore. Art is not nature, but rather nature digested. Art is a sublime excrement."

"And Daudet?" Balso queried.

"Oh, Daudet! Daudet, c'est de bouillabaisse! You know, George Moore also says, 'What care I that the virtue of some sixteen-year-old maiden was the price paid for Ingres' La Source?' Now . . ."

"Picasso says," Balso broke in, "Picasso says there are no feet in nature . . . And, thanks for showing me around. I have to leave."

But before he was able to get away, the guide caught him by the collar. "Just a minute, please. You were right to interrupt. We should talk of art, not artists. Please explain your interpretation of the Spanish master's dictum."

"Well, the point is . . ." Balso began. But before he could finish the guide started again. "If you are willing to acknowledge the existence of points," he said, "then the statement that there are no feet in nature puts you in an untenable position. It depends for its very meaning on the fact that there are no points. Picasso, by making this assertion, has placed himself on the side of monism in the eternal wrangle between the advocates of the Singular and those of the Plural. As James puts it, 'Does reality exist distributively or collectively—in the shape of *eaches, everys, anys, eithers* or only in the shape of an *all* or *whole?*' If reality is singular then there are no feet in nature, if plural, a great many. If the world is one [everything part of the same thing—called by Picasso nature] then nothing either begins or ends. Only when things take the shapes of *eaches, everys, anys, eithers* [have ends] do they have feet. Feet are attached to ends, by definition. Moreover, if everything is one, and has neither ends nor beginnings, then everything is a circle. A circle has neither a beginning nor an end. A circle has no feet. If we believe that nature is a circle, then we must also believe that there are no feet in nature.

"Do not pooh-pooh this idea as mystical. Bergson has . . ."

"Cezanne said, 'Everything tends toward the globular.'" With this announcement Balso made another desperate attempt to escape.

"Cezanne?" the guide said, keeping a firm hold on Balso's collar. "Cezanne is right. The sage of Aix is . . ."

With a violent twist, Balso tore loose and fled.

Balso fled down the great tunnel until he came upon a man, naked except for a derby in which thorns were stick-

ing, who was attempting to crucify himself with thumb
tacks. His curiosity got the better of his fear and he
stopped.

"Can I help you?" he asked politely.

"No," the man answered with even greater politeness,
tipping his hat repeatedly as he spoke. "No, I can manage,
thank you . . .

"My name is Maloney the Areopagite," the man continued, answering the questions Balso was too well-bred to
word, "and I am a catholic mystic. I believe implicitly in
that terrible statement of Saint Hildegarde's, 'The lord
dwells not in the bodies of the healthy and vigorous.' I
live as did Marie Alacoque, Suso, Labre, Lydwine of Schie-
dam, Rose of Lima. When my suffering is not too severe, I
compose verses in imitation of Notker Balbus, Ekkenard le
Vieux, Hucbald le Chauve.

"In the feathered darkness
Of thy mouth,
O Mother of God!
I worship Christ
The culminating rose.

"Get the idea? I spend the rest of my time marveling at
the love shown by all the great saints for even the lowliest
of God's creatures. Have you ever heard of Benedict Labre?
It was he who picked up the vermin that fell out of his hat
and placed them piously back into his sleeve. Before calling in a laundress, another very holy man removed the
vermin from his clothes in order not to drown the jewels of
sanctity infesting them.

"Inspired by these thoughts I have decided to write the
biography of Saint Puce, a great martyred member of the
vermin family. If you are interested, I will give you a short
précis of his life.

"Please do so, sir," Balso said. "Live and learn is my motto, Mr. Maloney, so please continue."

"Saint Puce was a flea," Maloney the Areopagite began in a well-trained voice. "A flea who was born, lived, and died, beneath the arm of our Lord.

"Saint Puce was born from an egg that was laid in the flesh of Christ while as a babe He played on the floor of the stable in Bethlehem. That the flesh of a god has been a stage in the incubation of more than one being is well known: Dionysius and Athene come to mind.

"Saint Puce had two mothers: the winged creature that laid the egg, and the God that hatched it in His flesh. Like most of us, he had two fathers: our Father Who art in Heaven, and he who in the cocksureness of our youth we called 'pop.'

"Which of his two fathers fertilized the egg? I cannot answer with certainty, but the subsequent actions of Saint Puce's life lead me to believe that the egg was fertilized by a being whose wings were of feathers. Yes, I mean the Dove or Paraclete—the Sanctus Spiritus. In defense of this belief antiquity will help us again: it is only necessary to remember Leda and Europa. And I must remind you, you who might plead a puce too small physically, of the nature of God's love and how it embraceth all.

"O happy, happy childhood! Playing in the curled brown silk, sheltered from all harm by Christ's arm. Eating the sweet flesh of our Saviour; drinking His blood; bathing in His sweat; partaking, oh how fully! of His Godhead. Having no need to cry as I have cried:

"Corpus Christi, salva me
Sanguis Christi, inebria me
Aqua lateris Christi, lave me.

"In manhood, fullgrown, how strong Saint Puce was, how lusty; and how his lust and strength were satisfied in one continuous, never-culminating ecstasy. The music of our Lord's skin sliding over His flesh!—more exact than the fugues of Bach. The pattern of His veins!—more intricate than the Maze at Cnossos. The odors of His Body!—more fragant than the Temple of Solomon. The temperature of His flesh!—more pleasant than the Roman baths to the youth Puce. And, finally, the taste of His blood! In this wine all pleasure, all excitement, was magnified, until with ecstasy Saint Puce's small body roared like a furnace.

"In his prime, Saint Puce wandered far from his birthplace, that hairsilk pocketbook, the armpit of our Lord. He roamed the forest of God's chest and crossed the hill of His abdomen. He measured and sounded that fathomless well, the Navel of our Lord. He explored and charted every crevasse, ridge, and cavern of Christ's body. From notes taken during his travels he later wrote his great work, *A Geography of Our Lord.*

"After much wandering, tired, he returned at last to his home in the savoury forest. To spend, he thought, his remaining days in writing, worship, and contemplation. Happy in a church whose walls were the flesh of Christ, whose windows were rose with the blood of Christ, and on whose altars burned golden candles made of the sacred earwax.

"Soon, too soon, alas! the day of martyrdom arrived [O Jesu, mi dulcissime!], and the arms of Christ were lifted that His hands might receive the nails.

"The walls and windows of Saint Puce's church were broken and its halls flooded with blood.

"The hot sun of Calvary burnt the flesh beneath Christ's upturned arm, making the petal-like skin shrivel until it looked like the much-shaven armpit of an old actress.

"After Christ died, Saint Puce died, refusing to desert to lesser flesh, even to that of Mary who stood close under the cross. With his last strength he fought off the unconquerable worm. . . ."

Mr. Maloney's thin frame was racked by sobs as he finished, yet Balso did not spare him.

"I think you're morbid," he said. "Don't be morbid. Take your eyes off your navel. Take your head from under your armpit. Stop sniffing mortality. Play games. Don't read so many books. Take cold showers. Eat more meat."

With these helpful words, Balso left him to his own devices and continued on his way.

He had left Maloney the Areopagite far behind when, on turning a bend in the intestine, he saw a boy hiding what looked like a packet of letters in a hollow tree. After the boy had left, Balso removed the packet and sat down to read. First, however, he took off his shoes because his feet hurt.

What he had taken for letters proved on closer scrutiny to be a diary. At the top of the first page was written, "English Theme by John Gilson, Class 8B, Public School 186, Miss McGeeney, teacher." He read further.

Jan. 1st—at home

Whom do I fool by calling these pages a journal? Surely not you, Miss McGeeney. Alas! no-one. Nor is anyone fooled by the fact that I write in the first person. It is for this reason that I do not claim to have found these pages in a hollow tree. I am an honest man and feel badly about masks, cardboard noses, diaries, memoirs, letters from a Sabine farm, the theatre . . . I feel badly, yet I can do nothing. 'Sir!' I say to myself, 'your name is not Iago, but simply John. It is monstrous to write lies in a diary.'

However, I insist that I am an honest man. Reality troubles me as it must all honest men.

Reality! Reality! If I could only discover the Real. A Real that I could know with my senses. A Real that would wait for me to inspect it as a dog inspects a dead rabbit. But, alas! when searching for the Real I throw a stone into a pool whose ripples become of advancing less importance until they are too large for connection with, or even memory of, the stone agent.

Written while smelling the moistened forefinger of my left hand.

Jan 2nd—at home

Is this journal to be like all the others I have started? A large first entry, consisting of the incident which made me think my life exciting enough to keep a journal, followed by a series of entries gradually decreasing in size and culminating in a week of blank days.

Inexperienced diary-writers make their first entry the largest. They come to the paper with a constipation of ideas—eager, impatient. The white paper acts as a laxative. A diarrhoea of words is the result. The richness of the flow is unnatural; it cannot be sustained.

A diary must grow naturally—a flower, a cancer, a civilization . . . In a diary there is no need for figures of speech, honest Iago.

Sometimes my name is Raskolnikov, sometimes it is Iago. I never was, and never shall be, plain John Gilson—honest, honest Iago, yes, but never honest John. As Raskolnikov, I

keep a journal which I call *The Making of a Fiend.* I give
the heart of my Crime Journal:

Crime Journal

I have been in this hospital seven weeks. I am under observation. Am I sane? This diary shall prove me insane.

This entry gives me away.

Crime Journal

My mother visited me today. She cried. It is she who is
crazy. Order is the test of sanity. Her emotions and
thoughts are disordered. Mine are arranged, valued, placed.

Man spends a great deal of time making order out of
chaos, yet insists that the emotions be disordered. I order
my emotions: I am insane. Yet sanity is discipline. My
mother rolls on the hospital floor and cries: "John darling
. . . John sweetheart." Her hat falls over face. She clutches
her absurd bag of oranges. She is sane.

I say to her quietly: "Mother, I love you, but this specta-
cle is preposterous—and the smell of your clothing de-
presses me." I am insane.

Crime Journal

Order is vanity. I have decided to discard the nonsense of
precision instruments. No more measuring. I drop the slide
rule and take up the Golden Rule. Sanity is the absence of
extremes.

Crime Journal

Is someone reading my diary while I sleep?

On reading what I have written, I think I can detect a
peculiar change in my words. They have taken on the quality of comment.

*You who read these pages while I sleep, please sign
your name here.*

John Raskolnikov Gilson

Crime Journal
During the night I got up, turned to yesterday's entry and signed my name.

Crime Journal
I am insane. I [the papers had it CULTURED FIEND SLAYS DISHWASHER] am insane.

When a baby, I affected all the customary poses: I "laughed the icy laughter of the soul," I uttered "universal sighs"; I sang in "silver-fire verse"; I smiled the "enigmatic smile"; I sought "azure and elliptical routes." In everything I was completely the mad poet. I was one of those "great despisers," whom Nietzche loved because "they are the great adorers; they are arrows of longing for the other shore." Along with "mon hysterie" I cultivated a "rotten, ripe maturity." You understand what I mean: like Rimbaud, I practiced having hallucinations.

Now, my imagination is a wild beast that cries always for freedom. I am continually tormented by the desire to indulge some strange thing, perceptible but indistinct, hidden in the swamps of my mind. This hidden thing is always crying out to me from its hiding-place: "Do as I tell you and you will find out my shape. There, quick! what is that thing in your brain? Indulge my commands and some day the great doors of your mind will swing open and allow you to enter and handle to your complete satisfaction the vague shapes and figures hidden there."

I can know nothing; I can have nothing; I must devote my whole life to the pursuit of a shadow. It is as if I were attempting to trace with the point of a pencil the shadow of the tracing pencil. I am enchanted with the shadow's shape and want very much to outline it; but the shadow is attached to the pencil and moves with it, never allowing me to trace its tempting form. Because of some great need, I am continually forced to make the attempt.

Two years ago I sorted books for eight hours a day in the public library. Can you imagine how it feels to be surrounded for eight long hours by books—a hundred billion words one after another according to ten thousand mad schemes. What patience, what labor are those crazy sequences the result of! What starving! What sacrifice! And the fervors, deliriums, ambitions, dreams, that dictated them! . . .

The books smelt like the breaths of their authors; the books smelt like a closet full of old shoes through which a steam pipe passes. As I handled them they seemed to turn into flesh, or at lest some substance that could be eaten.

Have you ever spent any time among the people who farm the great libraries: the people who search old issues of the medical journals for pornography and facts about strange diseases; the comic writers who exhume jokes from old magazines; the men and women employed by the insurance companies to gather statistics on death? I worked in the philosophy department. That department is patronized by alchemists, astrologers, cabalists, demonologists, magicians, atheists, and the founders of new religious systems.

While working in the library, I lived in a theatrical rooming house in the west Forties, a miserable, uncomfortable place. I lived there because of the discomfort. I wanted to be miserable. I could not have lived in a comfortable house. The noises [harsh, grating], the dirt [animal, greasy], the smells [dry sweat, sour mold], permitted me to wallow in my discomfort. My mind was full of vague irritations and annoyances. My body was nervous and jumpy, and demanded an extraordinary amount of sleep. I was a bundle of physical and mental tics. I climbed into myself like a bear into a hollow tree, and lay there long hours, overpowered by the heat, odor, and nastiness of I.

The only other person living on my floor, the top one,

was an idiot. He earned his living as a dishwasher in the kitchen of the Hotel Astor. He was a fat, pink and grey pig of a man, and stank of stale tobacco, dry perspiration, clothing mold, and oatmeal soap. He did not have a skull on the top of his neck, only a face; his head was all face—a face without side, back or top, like a mask.

The idiot never wore a collar, yet he kept both a front and a back collar button in the neckband of his shirt. When he changed his shirt he removed the collar buttons from the dirty shirt and placed them in the clean one. His neck was smooth, white, fat, and covered all over with tiny blue veins like a piece of cheap marble. His Adam's apple was very large and looked as though it might be a soft tumor in his throat. When he swallowed, his neck bulged out and he made a sound like a miniature toilet being flushed.

My neighbor, the idiot, never smiled, but laughed continually. It must have hurt him to laugh. He fought his laughter as though it were a wild beast. A beast of laughter seemed always struggling to escape from between his teeth.

People say that it is terrible to hear a man cry. I think it is even worse to hear a man laugh. [Yet the ancients considered hysteria a woman's disease. They believed that hysteria was caused by the womb breaking loose and floating freely through the body. The cure they practiced was to place sweet-smelling herbs to the vulva in order to attract the womb back to its original position, and foul-smelling things to the nose in order to keep the womb away from the head.]

One night at the movies, I heard a basso from the Chicago Opera Company sing the devil's serenade from Faust. A portion of this song calls for a long laugh. When the singer came to the laugh he was unable to get started. He struggled with the laugh, but it refused to come. At last he managed to start laughing. Once started, he was unable to stop. The orchestra repeated the transition that led from the laugh to the next bars of the song, but he was unable to stop laughing.

I returned home with my head full of the singer's laughter. Because of it I was unable to fall asleep. I dressed myself and went downstairs. On my way to the street I passed my neighbor the idiot. He was laughing to himself. His laughter made me laugh. When he detected the strain in my voice he grew angry. He thought that I was making fun of him. He said, "Who you laughing at?" I became frightened and offered him a cigarette. He refused it. I left him on the stairs, struggling with his laughter and his anger.

I knew that if I did not get my customary amount of sleep, I would suffer when the time came for me to get up. I was certain that if I went back to bed I would be unable to sleep. In order to tire myself as quickly as possible, I walked to Broadway and then started uptown. My shoes hurt me and at first I enjoyed the pain. Soon, however, the pain became so intense that I had to stop walking and return home.

On regaining my bed, I still found it impossible to fall asleep. I knew that I must become interested in something outside of myself or go insane. I plotted the death of the idiot.

I felt certain that it would be a safe murder to commit. Safe, because its motives would not be comprehensible to the police. Policemen are reasonable men; they do not consider the shape and color of a man's throat, his laugh or the fact that he does not wear a collar, reasonable motives for killing him.

You also, eh, doctor, consider these poor reasons for murder. I agree—they are literary reasons. Reasoning your way, dear doctor—like Darwin or a policeman—I am expected to trace my action back to some such things as the desire to live or create life. Because I want you to believe me, I shall say that in order to remain sane I had to kill this man, just as I had to kill, when a child, all the flies in my room before being able to fall asleep.

Nonsense, eh? I agree—nonsense. Please, please—here [please believe me] is why I killed Adolph. I killed the idiot because he disturbed my sense of balance. I killed him thinking his death would permit me to regain my balance. My beloved balance!

The fact that I had never killed made me uncomfortable. What was this enormous crime I had never committed? What were all the horrors attendant on this act? I killed a man and discovered the answers. I shall never kill another man. I shall never need to kill another man.

Let me continue with my confession. I decided not to plot an intricate killing. I was afraid that if I attempted a complicated crime I might get entangled in my own scheme. I decided to have the murder consist of only one act, the killing. I even resisted the desire to look up certain books in the library.

Because the idea of the killing involved the dishwasher's throat, I decided to do the job with a knife. As a child I always took pleasure in cutting soft, firm things. I purchased a knife about fifteen inches long. The knife had only one cutting edge; the other edge or the back of the knife was about half an inch thick. Its weight made it a perfect instrument for the job.

I did not want to commit the murder too soon after purchasing the knife; but on the very night that I brought it home, I heard the idiot come up the stairs drunk. As I listened to him fumble with his key, I realized, for the first time, that he locked his door at night. This unlooked-for obstacle almost made me give up the idea of killing him. I rid myself of my misgivings by thinking of the torture I would have to go through if I frustrated my desire to commit murder. I decided to do the job that very evening and have it over with. I put on my bathrobe and went into the hall. His door was ajar. I went to it carefully. The idiot was stretched out on his bed, drunk. I went back to my room and took off my bathrobe and pajamas. I planned to do the murder naked, so that I should have no blood-stained things to wash or destroy. What blood I got on my body I could easily wash off. Naked: I felt cold; and I noticed that my genitals were tight and hard, like a dog's, or an archaic Greek statue's—they were as though I had just come out of an ice-cold bath. I was aware of a great excitement; an excitement that seemed to be near, but not quite within me.

I crossed the hall and entered the dishwasher's room. He had left his light burning. I walked to him and cut his throat. I had intended to do the cutting with several rapid strokes, but he awoke at the touch of the steel and I became frightened and sawed at his throat in a panic. When he lay still I calmed down.

I went back to my room and stood the knife up in the sink, like one does a wet umbrella, letting what blood was on it run into the drain. I dressed quickly, obsessed by the need for getting rid of the knife. While dressing I became conscious of a growing fear. A fear that as it grew seemed likely to burst me open; a fear so large that I felt I could not contain it without rupturing my mind. Inside of my head this expanding fear was like a rapidly growing child inside the belly of a mother. I felt that I must get rid of the fear or burst. I opened my mouth wide, but I was unable to give birth to my fear.

Carrying this fear as an ant carries a caterpiller thirty times its size, I ran down the stairs and into the street. I hurried west toward the river.

I let the knife slip into the water. With the knife went my fear. I felt light and free. I felt like a happy girl. I said to myself: "You feel like a young girl—kittenish, cuneycutey, darlingey, springtimey." I caressed my breasts like a young girl who has suddenly become conscious of her body on a hot afternoon. I imitated the mannered walk of a girl showing off before a group of boys. In the dark I hugged myself.

On my way back to Broadway I passed some sailors, and felt an overwhelming desire to flirt with them. I went through all the postures of a desperate prostitute; I camped for all I was worth. The sailors looked at me and laughed. I wanted very much for one of them to follow me. Suddenly I heard the sound of footsteps behind me. The steps came close and I felt as though I were melting—all silk and perfumed, pink lace. I died the little death. But the man went past without noticing me. I sat down on a bench and was violently sick.

I sat on the bench for a long time, and then returned to my room, sick and cold.

Inside of my head the murder has become like a piece of sand inside the shell of an oyster. My mind has commenced to form a pearl around it. The idiot, the singer, his laugh, the knife, the river, my change of sex, all cover the murder just as the secretions of an oyster cover an irritating grain of sand. As the accumulations grow and become solidified, the original irritation disappears. If the murder continues to grow in size it may become too large for me to contain; then I am afraid it will kill me, just as the pearl eventually kills the oyster.

Balso put the manuscript back into the tree and continued on his way, his head bowed in thought. The world was getting to be a difficult place for a lyric poet. He felt old. "Ah youth!" he sighed elaborately. "Ah Balso Snell!"

Suddenly he heard a voice at his elbow.

"Well, nosey, how did you like my theme?"

Balso turned and saw the boy whose diary he had been reading. He was still in short pants and looked less than twelve years old.

"Interesting psychologically, but is it art?" Balso said timidly. "I'd give you B minus and a good spanking."

"What the hell do I care about art! Do you know why I wrote that ridiculous story—because Miss McGeeney, my English teacher, reads Russian novels and I want to sleep with her. But maybe you run a magazine. Will you buy it? I need money."

"No, son, I'm a poet. I'm Balso Snell, the poet."

"A poet! For Christ's sake!"

"What you ought to do, child, is to run about more. Read less and play baseball."

"Forget it. I know a fat girl who only sleeps with poets. When I'm with her I'm a poet, too. I won her with a poem.

"O Beast of Walls!
O Walled-in Fat Girl!
Your conquest was hardly worth
The while of one whom Arras and
Arrat, Pelion, Ossa, Parnassus, Ida,
Pisgah and Pike's Peak never in-
terested.

"Not bad, eh? But I'm fed up with poetry and art. Yet what can I do. I need women and because I can't buy or force them, I have to make poems for them. God knows how tired I am of using the insanity of Van Gogh and the adventures of Gauguin as can-openers for the ambitious Count Six-Times. And how sick I am of literary bitches. But they're the only kind that'll have me. . . . Listen, Balso, for a dollar I'll sell you a brief outline of my position."

Balso gave the dollar to get rid of him and received in return a little pamphlet.

THE PAMPHLET

Yesterday, while debating whether I should shave or not, news of the death of my friend Saniette arrived. I decided not to shave.

Today, while shaving, I searched myself for yesterday's emotions. Searched, that is, the pockets of my dressing gown and the shelves of the medicine closet. Not finding anything, I looked further. I looked [first smiling, of course] into the bowels of my compassion, the depths of my being, and even into the receding vistas of my memory. I came from my search, as was to be expected, empty-handed. My "Open, oh flood gates of feeling! Empty, oh vials of passion!" made certain and immediate the defeat of my purpose.

That I failed in my search was for me a sign of my intelligence. I am [just as children choose sides to play "cops and robbers" or "Indians and cowboys"] on the side of intellect against the emotions, on the side of the brain against the heart. Nevertheless, I recognized the cardboard and tin of my position [a young man, while shaving, dismisses Death with a wave of his hand] and did not give up my search for an emotion. I marshalled all my reasons for grief [I had lived with Saniette for almost two years], yet failed to find sorrow.

Death is a very difficult thing for me to consider sincerely because I find certain precomposed judgments awaiting my method of consideration to render it absurd. No matter how I form my comment I attach to it the criticisms sentimental, satirical, formal. With these judgments there goes a series of literary associations which remove me still further from genuine feeling. The very act of recognizing Death, Love, Beauty—all the major subjects—has become, from literature and exercise, impossible.

After admitting to myself that I had failed, I tried to cover my defeat by practicing a few sneers in the bathroom mirror. I remembered that yesterday I had used Saniette's death as an excuse for not shaving and added in a loud voice, "Just as more than one friend will use the occasion of my death as an excuse for breaking an undesired appointment."

Heartened by my sneering reflection in the mirror, I pictured the death of Saniette. Hiding under the blankets of her hospital bed and invoking the aid of Mother Eddy and Doctor Coué: "I won't die! I am getting better and better. I won't die! The will is master o'er the flesh. I won't die!" Only to have Death answer: "Oh, yes you will." And she had. I made Death's triumph my own.

The inevitability of death has always given me pleasure, not because I am eager to die, but because all the Saniettes must die. When the preacher explained the one thing all men could be certain of—all must die—the King of France became angry. When death prevailed over the optimism of Saniette, she was, I am certain, surprised. The thought of Saniette's surprise pleases me, just as the King's anger must have pleased the preacher.

Only a portion of my dislike for Saniette is based on the natural antipathy pessimists feel for optimists, cowboys for Indians, cops for robbers. For a large part it consists of that equally natural antipathy felt by the performer for his audience. My relations with Saniette were exactly those of performer and audience.

While living with me, Saniette accepted my most desperate feats in somewhat the manner one watches the marvelous stunts of acrobats. Her casualness excited me so that I became more and more desperate in my performances. A tragedy with only one death is nothing in the theatre—why not two deaths? Why not a hundred? With some such idea as this in mind I exhibited my innermost organs: I wore my heart and genitals around my neck. At each exhibition I watched carefully to see how she received my performance—with a smile or with a tear. Though I exhibited myself as a clown, I wanted no mistakes to be made; I was a tragic clown.

I have forgotten the time when I could look back at an affair with a woman and remember anything but a sequence of theatrical poses—poses that I assumed, no matter how aware I was of their ridiculousness, because they were amusing. All my acting has but one purpose, the attraction of the female.

If it had been possible for me to attract by exhibiting a series of physical charms, my hatred would have been less. But I found it necessary to substitute strange conceits, wise and witty sayings, peculiar conduct, Art, for the muscles, teeth, hair, of my rivals.

All this much-exhibited intelligence is but a development of the instinct to please. My case is similar to that of a bird called the Amblyornis inornata. As his name indicates, the Inornata is a dull-colored, ugly bird. Yet the Inornata is cousin to the Bird of Paradise. Because he lacks his cousin's brilliant plumage, he has to exteriorize internal feathers. The Inornata plants a garden and builds a house of flowers as a substitute for the gay feathers of his relative. Of course the female Inornata loves her shabby artist dearly; yet when a friend passes, Mrs. Bird of Paradise can say, "Show your tail, dear," while Mrs. Inornata, to her confusion, has no explanation to give for her love. If she is in a temper she might even ask Mr. Inornata to exteriorize a few internal feathers. Still more, the Bird of

Paradise cannot be blamed for the quality of his tail—it just grew. The Inornata, however, is held personally responsible for his performance as an artist.

There was a time when I felt that I was indeed a rare spirit. Then I had genuinely expressed my personality with a babe's delight in confessing the details of its inner life. Soon, however, in order to interest my listeners, I found it necessary to shorten my long outpourings; to make them, by straining my imagination, spectacular. Oh, how much work goes into the search for the odd, the escape from the same!

Because of women like Saniette, I acquired the habit of extravagant thought. I now convert everything into fantastic entertainment and the extraordinary has become an obsession. . . .

An intelligent man finds it easy to laugh at himself, but his laughter is not sincere if it is thorough. If I could be Hamlet, or even a clown with a breaking heart 'neath his jester's motley, the role would be tolerable. But I always find it necessary to burlesque the mystery of feeling at its source; I must laugh at myself, and if the laugh is "bitter," I must laugh at the laugh. The ritual of feeling demands burlesque and, whether the burlesque is successful or not, a laugh. . . .

One night, while in a hotel bedroom with Saniette, I grew miserably sick of the mad dreams I had been describing to amuse her. I began to beat her. While beating her, I was unable to forget that strange man, John Raskolnikov Gilson, the Russian student. As I beat her, I shouted: "O constipation of desire! O diarrhoea of love! O life within life! O mystery of being! O Young Women's Christian Association! Oh! Oh!"

When her screams brought the hotel clerk to our door,

I attempted to explain my irritation. In part I said: "This evening I am very nervous. I have a sty on my eye, a cold sore on my lip, a pimple where the edge of my collar touches my neck, another pimple in the corner of my mouth, and a drop of salt snot on the end of my nose. Because I rub them continually my nostrils are inflamed, sore and angry.

"My forehead is wrinkled so hard that it hurts, yet I cannot unwrinkle it. I spend many hours trying to unwrinkle my forehead. I try to catch myself by surprise; I try to smooth my forehead with my fingers; I try to concentrate my whole mind to this end, but I am unable to make smooth my brow. The skin over my eyebrows is tied in an aching, unbreakable knot.

"The wood of this table, the glasses on it, this girl's woollen dress, the skin under it, excites and annoys me. It seems to me as though all the materials of life—wood, glass, wool, skin—are rubbing against my sty, my cold sore and my pimples; rubbing in such a way as not to satisfy the itch or convert irritation into active pain, but so as to increase the size of the irritation, magnify it and make it seem to cover everything—hysteria, despair.

"I go to a mirror and squeeze the sty with all my strength. I tear off the cold sore with my nails. I scrub my salt-encrusted nostrils with the rough sleeve of my overcoat. If I could only turn irritation into pain; could push the whole thing into insanity and so escape. I am able to turn irritation into active pain for only a few seconds, but the pain soon subsides and the monotonous rhythm of irritation returns. O how fleeting is pain!—I cry. I think of sandpapering my body. I think of grease, of sandalwood oil, of saliva; I think of velvet, of Keats, of music, of the hardness of precious stones, of mathematics, of the arrangements of architecture. But, alas! I can find no relief."

Both Saniette and the clerk refused to understand. Saniette said that she understood the irritation I was talking about was one of the spirit; yet, she added, the only conclusion she could arrive at—a gentleman would never strike a lady—was that I no longer loved her. The clerk murmured something about the police.

In order to get him away from the door, I asked him if he had ever heard of the Marquis de Sade or of Gilles de Rais. Fortunately, we were in a Broadway hotel whose employees are familiar with the world. When I mentioned these names, the clerk bowed and left us with a smile. Saniette was also of the world; she smiled and went back to bed.

The next morning, remembering their smiles, I thought it advisable to explain my actions again. Not that it was necessary for me to differentiate between the kind of a beating alcohol inspires a temperance-cartoon drunkard to give his hard-working spouse, and the beating I had given Saniette; but, rather, that I found it difficult to illustrate the point I desired to make clear.

"When you think of me, Saniette," I said, "think of two men—myself and the chauffeur within me. This chauffeur is very large and dressed in ugly ready-made clothing. His shoes, soiled from walking about the streets of a great city, are covered with animal ordure and chewing gum. His hands are covered with coarse woollen gloves. On his head is a derby hat.

"The name of this chauffeur is The Desire to Procreate.

"He sits within me like a man in an automobile. His heels are in my bowels, his knees on my heart, his face in my brain. His gloved hands hold me firmly by the tongue; his hands, covered with wool, refuse me speech for the emotions aroused by the face in my brain.

"From within, he governs the sensations I receive through my fingers, eyes, tongue and ears.

"Can you imagine how it feels to have this cloth-covered devil within one? While naked, were you ever embraced by a fully clothed man? Do you remember how his button-covered coat felt, how his heavy shoes felt against your skin? Imagine having this man inside of you, fumbling and fingering your heart and tongue with wool-covered hands, treading your tender organs with stumbling soiled feet."

Because of the phrasing of my complaint, Saniette was able to turn my revenge into a joke. She weathered a second beating with a slow, kind smile.

Saniette represents a distinct type of audience—smart, sophisticated, sensitive yet hardboiled, art-loving frequenters of the little theatres. I am their particular kind of a performer.

Some day I shall obtain my revenge by writing a play for one of their art theatres. A theatre patronized by the discriminating few: art-lovers and book-lovers, school teachers who adore the grass-eating Shaw, sensitive young Jews who adore culture, lending librarians, publisher's assistants, homosexualists and homosexualists' assistants, hard-drinking newpaper men, interior decorators, and the writers of advertising copy.

In this play I shall take my beloved patrons into my confidence and flatter their difference from other theatre-goers. I shall congratulate them on their good taste in preferring Art to animal acts. Then, suddenly, in the midst of some very witty dialogue, the entire cast will walk to the footlights and shout Chekov's advice:

"It would be more profitable for the farmer to raise rats for the granary than for the bourgeois to nourish the artist, who must always be occupied with undermining institutions."

In case the audience should misunderstand and align

itself on the side of the artist, the ceiling of the theatre will be made to open and cover the occupants with tons of loose excrement. After the deluge, if they so desire, the patrons of my art can gather in the customary charming groups and discuss the play.

When he had finished reading, Balso threw the pamphlet away with a sigh. In his childhood, things had been managed differently; besides, shaving had not been permitted before the age of sixteen. Having no alternative, Balso blamed the war, the invention of printing, nineteenth-century science, communism, the wearing of soft hats, the use of contraceptives, the large number of delicatessen stores, the movies, the tabloids, the lack of adequate ventilation in large cities, the passing of the saloon, the soft collar fad, the spread of foreign art, the decline of the western world, commercialism, and, finally, for throwing the artist back on his own personality, the renaissance.

"What is beauty saith my sufferings then?" asked Balso of himself, quoting Marlowe.

As though in answer to his question, he saw standing naked before him a slim young girl busily washing her hidden charms in a public fountain. Through the wood of his brain there buzzed the saw of desire.

She called to him, saying:

"Charge, oh poet, the red-veined flowers of suddenly remembered intimacies—the foliage of memory. Feel, oh poet, the warm knife of thought swift stride and slit in the ready garden.

"Soon the hot seed will come to thwart the knife's progress. The hot seed will come in a joyous burst-birth of reeking undergrowth and swamp forest.

"Walk toward the houses of the city of your memory, oh poet! Houses that are protuberances on the skin of streets—warts, tumors, pimples, corns, nipples, sebaceous cysts, hard and soft chancres.

"Like the gums of false teeth, red are the signs imploring you to enter the game paths lit by iron flowers. Like ants under a new-turned stone, hysterical are the women who run there clad in the silk tights of pleasure, oiled with fish slime. Women whose only delight is to rub the jaded until it becomes irritated and grows new things, pimples of a . . ."

Throwing his arms around her, Balso interrupted her recitation by sticking his tongue into her mouth. But when he closed his eyes to heighten the fun, he felt that he was embracing tweed. He opened them and saw that what he held in his arms was a middle aged woman dressed in a mannish suit and wearing hornrimmed glasses.

"My name is Miss McGeeney," she said. "I am a writer as well as a school teacher. Let's discuss something."

Balso wanted to bash her jaw in, but he found that he could not move. He tried to curse, but could only say: "How interesting. On what are you working?"

"At present I am writing a biography of Samuel Perkins. Stark, clever, disillusioned stuff, with a tenderness devoid of sentiment, yet touched by pity and laughter and irony. Into this book I hope to put the whimsical humor, the kindly satire of a mellow life.

"On the surface *Samuel Perkins: Smeller* [for so I call it] is simply a delightful story for children. The discriminating adult soon discovers, however, that it sprang from the brain of a kindly philosopher, that it is a genial satire on humanity.

"Under the title I intend placing as motto a verse from Juvenal: 'Who is surprised to see a goiter in the Alps? Quis tumidum guttur miratur in Alpibus?' I feel that this quotation strikes the keynote of the work.

"But who is Samuel Perkins, you are probably wondering. Samuel Perkins is the biographer of E. F. Fitzgerald. And who is Fitzgerald? You are of course familiar with D. B. Hobson's life of Boswell. Well, E. F. Fitzgerald is the author of a life of Hobson. The subject of my biography, Samuel Perkins, wrote a life of Fitzgerald.

"Sometime ago, a publisher asked me to write a biography, and I decided to do one of E. F. Fitzgerald. Fortunately, before commencing my study, I met Samuel Perkins who told me that he had written a biography of Fitzgerald the biographer of Hobson the biographer of Boswell. This news did not discourge me, but, on the contrary, made me determine to write a life of Perkins and so become another link in a brilliant literary chain. It seems to me that someone must surely take the hint and write the life of Miss McGreeney, the woman who wrote the biography of the man who wrote the biography of the man who wrote the biography of the man who wrote the biography of Boswell. And that, ad infinitum, we will all go rattling down the halls of time, each one in his or her turn a tin can on the tail of Doctor Johnson.

"But there are other good reasons for writing a life of Perkins. He was a great, if peculiar, genius with a character that lends itself most readily to biography.

"At an age when most men's features are regular, before his personality had been able to elevate any one portion of his physiognomy over the rest, Perkins' face was dominated by his nose. This fact I have ascertained from a collection of early photographs lent me by a profound admirer of Perkins and a fellow practitioner of his art. I refer to Robert Jones, author of a book called *Nosologie*.

"When I met Perkins for the first time, his face reminded me of the body of a man I had known at college. According to gossip current in the girls' dormitory this man abused himself. The source of these rumors lay in the peculiar shape of his body: all the veins, muscles and sinews flowed toward and converged at one point. In a like manner the wrinkles on Perkins' face, the contours of his head, the lines of his brow and chin, seemed to have melted and run into his nose.

"At this first meeting, Perkins said something that was later to prove very illuminating. He quoted Lucretius to the effect that 'his nose was quicker to scent a fetid sore or a rank armpit, than a dog to smell out the hidden sow.' Like most quotations, this one is only partially true. True, that is, of only one stage in Perkins' aesthetic development—the, what I have called quite arbitrarily, excrement period.

"It is possible to explain the powers of Perkins' magnificent sense of smell by the well-known theory of natural compensation. No one who has ever observed the acuteness of touch exhibited by a blind man or the gigantic shoulders of a legless man, will question the fact that Nature compensates for the loss of one attribute by lavishing her bounty on another. And Nature had made in the person of Samuel Perkins another attempt at justice. He was deaf and almost blind; his fingers fumbled stupidly; his mouth was always dry and contained a dull, insensitive tongue. But his nose! His nose was a marvelously sensitive and nice instrument. Nature had concentrated in his sense of smell all the abilities usually distributed among the five senses. She had strengthened this organ and had made it so sensitive that it was able to do duty for all the contact organs. Perkins was able to translate the sensations, sound, sight, taste, and touch, into that of smell. He could smell a chord in D minor, or distinguish between the tone-smell of a violin and that of a viola. He could smell the caress of velvet and the strength of iron. It has been said of him that he could smell an isosceles triangle; I mean that he could apprehend through the sense of smell the principles involved in isosceles triangles.

"In the ability to interpret the functions of one sense in terms of another, he is not alone. A French poet, in a sonnet of the vowels, called the letter I red and the letter U blue. Another symbolist, Father Castel, made a clavichord on which he was able to play melody and harmony by using color. Des Esseintes, Huysmans' hero, used a taste organ on which he composed symphonies for the palate.

"But can you imagine, new-found friend and esteemed poet, how horrible was the predicament of this sensitive and sensuous man forced to interpret the whole external world through conclusions reached by the sense of smell alone? If we have great difficulty in discovering the Real, how much greater must his difficulty have been?

"In my presence, Perkins once called the senses a tread-mill. 'A tread-mill,' he said, 'on which one can go only from the odors of Indian-grass baskets to the sour smells of Africa and the stinks of decay.'

"Rather than a tread-mill, I should call the senses a circle. A step forward along the circumference of a circle is a step nearer the starting place. Perkins went, along the circumference of the circle of his senses, from anticipation to realization, from hunger to satiation, from naïveté to sophistication, from simplicity to perversion. He went [speaking in Perkinsesque] from the smell of new-mown hay to that of musk and vervain [from the primitive to the romantic], and from vervain to sweat and excrement [from the romantic to the realistic]; and, finally, to complete the circuit, from excrement he returned to new-mown hay.

"There is, however, a way out for the artist and Perkins discovered it. The circumference of a circle infinite in size is a straight line. And a man like Perkins is able to make the circle of his sensory experience approach the infinite. He can so qualify the step from simplicity to perversion, for example, that the curve which makes inevitable the return to simplicity is imperceptible.

"One day Perkins told me that he was going to be married. I asked him if he thought his wife would understand him, and whether he thought he could be happy with a woman. He answered no to both questions, and said that he was marrying as an artist. I asked him to explain. He replied that the man who had numbered the smells of the human body and found them to be seven was a fool, unless the number was used in its mystic sense.

"After studying this strange conversation with the master, I discovered his meaning. He had found in the odors of a woman's body, never-ending, ever-fresh variation and change—a world of dreams, seas, roads, forests, textures, colors, flavors, forms. On my questioning him further, he confirmed my interpretation. He told me that he had built from the odors of his wife's body an architecture and an aesthetic, a music and a mathematic. Counterpoint, multiplication, the square of a sensation, the cube root of an experience—all were there. He told me that he had even discovered a politic, a hierarchy of odors: self-government, direct . . . "

By this time, Balso had gotten one of his hands free. He hit Miss McGeeney a terrific blow in the gut and hove her into the fountain.

The wooden horse, Balso realized as he walked on, was in-
habited solely by writers in search of an audience, and he
was determined not to be tricked into listening to another
story. If one had to be told, he would tell it.

As he hurried down the seemingly endless corridor, he
began to wonder whether he would ever reach the Anus
Mirabilis again. His feet hurt badly and his head ached.
When he came to a café built into the side of the intestine,
he sat down and ordered a glass of beer. After drinking
the beer, he took a newspaper out of his pocket, put it
over his face and went to sleep.

Balso dreamt that he was a young man again, lurking in
a corner of the Carnegie Hall lobby among the assembled
friends and relatives of music. The lobby was crowded
with the many beautiful girl-cripples who congregate
there because Art is their only solace, most men looking
upon their strange forms with distaste. But it was otherwise with Balso Snell. He likened their disarranged hips,
their short legs, their humps, their splay feet, their wall-
eyes, to ornament. Their strange foreshortenings, hanging
heads, bulging spinesacks, were a delight, for he had ever
preferred the imperfect, knowing well the plainness, the
niceness of perfection.

Spying a beautiful hunchback, he suddenly became sick
with passion. The cripple of his choice looked like some
creature from the depths of the sea. She was tall and
extraordinarily hunched. She was tall in spite of her

enormous hump; but for her dog-leg spine she would have been seven feet high. Moreover, he could be certain that, like all hunchbacks, she was intelligent.

He tipped his hat to her. She smiled and he snatched her from the throng, crying as he took her arm:

"O arabesque, I, Balso Snell, shall replace music in your affections! Your pleasures shall no longer be vicarious. No longer shall you mentally pollute yourself. For me, your sores are like flowers: the new, pink, budlike sores, the full, rose-ripe sores, the sweet, seed-bearing sores. I shall cherish them all. O deviation from the Golden Mean! O out of alignment!"

The Lepi [for so did he instantly dub her] opened her mouth to reply and exhibited one hundred and forty-four exquisite teeth in rows of four.

"Balso," she said, "you are a villian. Do you love as do all villains?"

"No," he answered, "I love only this." As he spoke, he laid his cool white hands upon her beautiful, hydrocephalic forehead. Then, bending over her enormous hump, he kissed her full on the brow.

Feeling his lips on her forehead, Janey Davenport, [the Lepi] gazed out over the blue waves of the Mediterranean and felt the delight of being young, rich, beautiful. No-one had ever before forgotten her strange shape long enough to realize how beautiful her soul was. She had never before known the thrill of being subdued by a male from a different land from that of her dreams. Now she had found a wonderful poet; now she knew the thrill she had never known before . . . had found it in the strength of this young and tall, strangely wise man, caught like herself in the meshes of the greatest net human hearts can know: Love.

Balso took her home and, in the hallway of her house, tried to seduce her. She allowed him one kiss, then broke away. From her lips—overhung by a moist eye and underhung by a heaving embonpoint—there came, "Love is a strange thing, is it not, Balso Snell?" He was afraid to laugh; he knew that if he even smiled the jig would be up. "Love," she said, "is beautiful. You, Balso, do not love. Love is sacred. How can you kiss if you do not love?" When he began to unbutton, she said with a desperately gay smile: "Would you want some one to ask of your sister what you ask of me? So this is why you invited me to dinner? I prefer music."

He made another attempt, but she fended him off. "Love," she began again, "Love, with me, Mr. Snell, is sacred. I shall never debase love, or myself, or the memory of my mother, in a hallway. Act your education, Mr. Snell. Tumbling in hallways at my age! How can you? After all, there are the eternal verities, not to speak of the janitor. And besides, we were never properly introduced."

After half an hour's sparring, he managed to warm her up a bit. She held him to her tightly for a second, capsized her eyeballs, and said: "If you only loved me, Balso. If you only loved me." He looked her in the eye, stroked her hump, kissed her brow, protesting desperately: "But I do love you, Janey. I do. I do. I swear it. I must have you. I must! I must!" She shoved him away with a sad yet determined smile. "First you will have to prove your love as did the knights of old."

"I'm ready," Balso cried. "What would you have me do?"

"Come inside and I'll tell you."

Balso followed her into the apartment and sat down beside her on a couch.

"I want you to kill a man called Beagle Darwin," she said with great firmness. "He betrayed me. In this hump on my back I carry his child. After you have killed him, I shall yield up my pink and white body to you, and then commit suicide."

"A bargain," Balso said. "Give me but your stocking to wear around my hat and I'm off to earn the prize."

"Not so fast, my gallant; first I must explain a few things to you.

"After listening to Beagle Darwin recite some of his poetry, I slept with him one night while my folks were visiting friends in Plainfield, New Jersey. Unfamiliar as I was with the wiles of men, I believed him when he told me that he loved me and wanted to take me to Paris to live in an artistic studio. I was very happy until I received the following letter."

Here the Lepi went to a bureau and took out two letters, one of which she gave Balso to read.

Darling Janey:

You persist in misunderstanding me. Please understand this: It is for your own good that I am refusing to take you to Paris, as I am firmly convinced that such a trip can only result in your death.

Here is the way in which you would die:

In your pajamas, Janey, you sit near the window and listen to the gay clatter of Paris traffic. The highpitched automobile horns make of every day a holiday. You are miserable.

You tell yourself: Oh, the carnival crowds are always hurrying past my window. I'm like an old actor mumbling Macbeth as he fumbles in the garbage can outside the theatre of his past triumphs. Only I'm not old; I'm young. Young, and I never had any triumphs to mumble over; my only triumphs were those I dreamed of having. I'm Janey Davenport, pregnant, unmarried, unloved, lonely, watching the laughing crowds hurry past her window.

I don't fit into life. I don't fit into his life. He only tolerates me for my body. He only wants one thing from me, and I want, oh how I want, love.

The ridiculous, the ridiculous, all day long he talks of nothing else but how ridiculous this, that, or the other thing is. And he means me. I am absurd. He is never satisfied with calling other people ridiculous, with him everything is ridiculous—himself, me. Of course I can laugh at Mother with him, or at the Hearth; but why must my own mother and home be ridiculous? I can laugh at Hobey, Joan, but I don't want to laugh at myself. I'm tired of laugh, laugh, laugh. I want to retain some portion of myself unlaughed at. There is something in me that I won't laugh at. I won't. I'll laugh at the outside world all he wants me to, but I won't, I don't want to laugh at my inner world. It's all right for him to say: "Be hard! Be an intellectual! Think, don't feel!" But I want to be soft. I want to feel. I don't want to think. I feel blue when I think. I want to keep a hard, outside surface towards the world, and a soft, inner side for him. And I want him to do the same, so that we can be secure in each other's love. But with his rotten, ugly jokes he keeps me at arm's length just when I want to be confiding and tender. When I show him my soft side he laughs. I don't want to be always on my guard against his laughter. There are times when I want to put down my armor. I am tired of eternally bearing armor against the world. Love is a merging, not an occasion for intellectual warfare. I want to enjoy my emotions. I want, sometimes, to play the child, and to make love like a child—tenderly, confidingly, prettily. I'm sick of his taunts.

Pregnant, unmarried, and he won't marry me. If I ask him to, he will laugh his terrible horse-laugh: "Well, my little bohemian, you want to get out of it, do you? Life, however, is Life; and the Realities are the Realities. You can't have your cake and eat it too, you know." He'll tell his friends the story as a joke—one of his unexplainable jokes. All his smug-faced friends will laugh at me, especially the Paige girl.

They don't like me; I don't fit in. All my life I have been a misfit—misunderstood. The carnival crowds are always hurrying past my window. As a kid, I never liked to play in the streets with the other kids; I always wanted to stay in the house and read a book. Since my father's death, I have no one to go to with my misery. He was always willing to understand and comfort me. Oh, how I want to be understood by someone who really loves me. Mother, like Beagle, always laughs at me. If they want to be kind it is, "You silly goose!" If they are angry, "Don't be an idiot." Only father was sympathetic, and he is dead. I wish I were dead.

Joan Higgins would know what to do if she were in my position—pregnant and unmarried. Joan fits into the kind of a life he and his friends lead better than I do. Like the time Joan said she had gone back to live with Hobey because it was such a bore looking for healthy men to sleep with. Joan warned me against him; she said he wasn't my kind. I thought him just my kind, sad and a poet. He is sad, but with a nasty sadness—all jeers for his own sadness. "It's the war. Everybody is sad nowadays. Great stuff, pessimism." Still he is sad; if he would only stop acting we could be very happy together. I want so much to comfort him—mother him.

Joan's advice would probably be for me to make him marry me. How he would howl. "Make an honest girl of you, eh?"

You can see the Café Carcas from the window. You are living in the Rue de la Grande Chaumiere, at the Hotel Liberia.

Why don't I fit in well at the Carcas? Joan would go big there. Why don't they like me? I'm as good looking as she is, and as clever. It's because I don't let myself go the way she does. Well, I don't want to. There is something fine in me that won't let me degrade myself.

You see me come out of the café, laughing and waving my arms.

I hope he comes upstairs.

You see me turn, and come towards the hotel.

Just as soon as he comes in I'll tell him I'm pregnant. I'll tell him in a matter-of-fact voice—casually. As long as I keep my tone casual he won't be able to laugh.

"Hello darling, how are you this morning?"
"All right. Beagle, je suis enceinte."
"You're what?"
[Oh, damn my pronunciation, I spoilt it.] "I'm pregnant." Despite your desire to appear casual you let a note of heartbreak into your voice. You droop.
"We'll have a party tonight and celebrate." I leave the room, shutting the door behind me, carefully.
Perhaps he'll never come back . . . You run to the window—sick. You sit down and prepare to indulge your misery. Your misery, your misery—you roll, you grovel in it. I'm pregnant! I'm pregnant! I'm pregnant! You force the rhythm of this cry into your blood. After the first moments of hysterical anguish are over, you wrap your predicament around you, snuggling into it, letting it cover you completely like a blanket. Your big trouble shelters you from a host of minor troubles. You are so miserable.

You remember that "life is a prison without bars," and think of suicide.

No one ever listens to me when I talk of suicide. The night I woke up in bed with him, it was no different. He thought I was joking when I said that I had frightened myself by brooding on death. But I told the truth. Death and suicide are never far from my thoughts. I said that death is like putting on a wet bathing suit. Now death seems warm and friendly. No, death is still like putting on a wet suit—shivery.

If I do it, I won't leave a note behind for him to laugh at. Just end it, that's all. No matter how I word a farewell note he will find something to laugh at—something to show his friends as a joke . . .

Mother knows I'm living with a man in Paris. Sophie wrote that everybody is talking about me. If I were to go home—even if I were not pregnant—mother would make an awful stink. I don't want to go back to the States: a long dull trip followed by a long dull life teaching elementary school.

What can I expect from him? He'll want me to have an abortion. They say that on account of the decreasing birth rate it is hard to get a competent doctor to do the operation. The French police are very strict. If the doctor killed me . . .

If I kill myself, I kill my body. I don't want to destroy my body; it is a good body—soft, white, and kind to me— a beautiful, happy body. If he were a true poet he would love me for my body's beauty; but he is like all men; he wants only one thing. Soon my body will be swollen and clumsy. The milk spoils the shape of a woman's breasts after an abortion. When my body becomes ugly, he will hate me. I once hoped that having a child would draw him closer to me—make him love me as a mother. But mother for him is always Mammy: a popular Broadway ballad, Mammy, Mammy, my old Kentucky Home, put it all together, it spells Mother. He doesn't see that Mother can mean shelter, love, intimacy. Oh, how much I want, I need, love.

If I wanted to make a squawk, mother would force him to marry me; but she would scold terribly and make a horrible scene. I'm too tired and sick to go through with a shotgun wedding.

Maybe I passed my period because of the wine—no, I know. Where did I read, "In my belly there is a tangled forest of arms and legs." It sounds like his stuff. When he left, he said he'd give a party tonight in honor of the occasion. I know what kind of a party it will be. He'll get drunk and make a speech: "Big with child, great with young—let me toast your gut, my dear. Here's to the pup! Waiters, stand erect while I toast my heir." He and his friends will expect me to join in the sport—to be a good sport.

He claims that the only place to commit suicide is on Chekov's grave. The Seine is also famous for suicide: " 'midst the bustle of 'Gay Paree'—suicide." "She killed herself in Paris." There is something tragic in the very thought. French windows make it easy; all you have to do is open the window and walk out. Every window over the third floor is a door into heaven. When I arrive there I can plead my belly—oh, how bitterly cruel the jest is. "Jest?" He would correct me—"not 'jest,' my dear, but joke; never, never say 'jest.' "

Oh, how miserable I am. I need love; I can't live without someone to treasure and comfort me. If I jumped from the third floor I might cripple myself—lucky this room is on the fourth. Lucky? [Animals never commit suicide.]

And mother—what would mother say? Mother would

feel worse about my being unmarried than about my death. I could leave a note asking him, as a final favor, to write her and say that we were married. He would forget to write.

When I'm dead, I'll be out of it all. Mother, Beagle—they will leave me alone. But I can't blame my trouble on him. I got myself into this mess. I went to his room after he acted decently in mine. I was jealous of Joan; she had so much fun going to men's rooms, and all that sort of thing. How childish Joan and her follies seem to me now.

When I'm dead the whole world as far as I am concerned—Beagle, mother—will be dead also. Or aussi: I came to Paris to learn French. I certainly learnt French. I wasn't even able to tell him in French without turning my trouble into a joke.

What love and a child by the man I loved once meant to me—and to live in Paris. If he should come back suddenly and catch me like this, brooding at the window, he'd say: "A good chance for you to kill two birds with one stone, my dear; but remember, an egg in the belly is worth more than a bird in the bush." What a pig he is! He thinks I haven't the nerve to kill myself. He patronizes me as though I were a child. "Suicide," he says, "is a charming affectation on the part of a young Russian, but in you, dear Janey, it is absurd."

You scream with irritation: "I'm serious! I am! I am! I don't want to live! I'm miserable! I don't want to live!"

I'm only teasing myself with thoughts of suicide at an open window. I know I won't do it. Mother will call me away: "Go away from that window—fool! You'll catch your death-cold or fall out—clumsy!"

At the word "clumsy" you fall to your death in the gutter below the window.

Horrible, eh? Yes, Janey, it is a suicide's grave that I saved you from when I refused to take you to Paris.

Yours,

Beagle

When Balso had finished reading, she handed him the other letter.

Darling Janey:

You did not take offence, I hope, at my letter. Please believe me when I say that I tried to make my treatment of your suicide as impersonal as possible. I did my best to keep the description of both our characters scientific and just. If I treated you savagely, I treated myself no gentler. It is true that I concentrated on you, but only because it was your suicide. In this letter I shall try to show, and so even the score, how I would have received your death.

You once said to me that I talk like a man in a book. I not only talk, but think and feel like one. I have spent my life in books; literature has deeply dyed my brain its own color. This literary coloring is a protective one—like the brown of the rabbit or the checks of the quail—making it impossible for me to tell where literature ends and I begin.

I start where I left off in my last letter:

As Janey's half-naked body crashed into the street, the usual crowds were hurrying to lunch from the Academies Colorossa and Grande Chaumiere; the concierge was coming out of the hotel's side door. In order to avoid running over her body, the driver of a cab coming from the Rue Notre Dame des Champs and going toward the Square de la Grande Chaumiere, brought his machine to a stop with screaming brakes. The concierge, on seeing the cab stop suddenly, one wheel over the body of a tenant of his, ran up, caught the chauffeur by the arm, and called loudly for the police. No one had seen her fall but the driver of the cab; he, bursting with rage, called the concierge an idiot, and pointed to the open window from which she had jumped. A crowd gathered around the chauffeur and shouted at him angrily. A policeman arrived. He, too, refused to believe the cab-driver, although he noticed that the dead girl was in her pajamas. "What would she be doing in the street in her night-clothes if she hadn't fallen from the window?" He shrugged his shoulders: "These American art students."

Beagle, on his way to the Café Carcas for a drink, turned to see where so many people were running. He saw the gesticulating group around the cab and went back, grateful for any diversion on what had been such a dull morning. As he joined them he kept thinking of Janey's announcement. "I'm pregnant." It reminded him of another announcement of hers. "It's about time I took a lover." "I'm pregnant" demanded for an answer, Life, just as "It's about time I took a lover" had been worthy of no less a reply than Love. She made a habit of these startling declarations: a few words, but freighted with meaning.

He knew what "I'm pregnant" meant; it meant canvassing his friends for the whereabouts of a doctor willing to perform the operation and writing frantic letters to the States for the necessary money. Through it all, Janey, having thrown the responsibility on him, would sit in one corner of the room: "Do with me what you will"—the groaning, patient, all-suffering, all-knowing, what has to be will be, beast of many burdens.

As he pushed into the crowd, someone told him a girl had been killed. He looked where the chauffeur was pointing and saw the open window of their room. Then he saw

Janey under the cab; he could not see her face, but he recognized her pajamas.

This was indeed a solution. The problem had been solved for him with a vengeance. He turned away and hurried up the street, afraid of being recognized. It had become impossible for him to take his drink at the Carcas. If he went there some friend would surely come to him with the news: "Beagle! Beagle! Janey has killed herself." He wanted to go somewhere and prepare a reply. "Here today and gone tomorrow" would never do, even at the Carcas.

He went past the Carcas up the Rue Delambre to the Avenue de Maine. On this street he went into a café hardly ever visited by Americans and sat down at a table in the corner of an inside room. He called for some cognac and asked himself:

Of what assistance could I have been? Should I have gone down on my knees in the street and wept over her dead body? Torn my hair? Called on the Deity? Or should I gave gone calmly up to the policeman and said: "I'm her husband. Allow me to accompany you to the morgue."

He ordered another cognac—Beagle Darwin the Destroyer. He pulled his hat down over his eyes and tossed off his drink.

She did it because she was pregnant. I would have married her, the fool. I hurt her when I made believe I didn't understand her French. "Je suis enceinte." My "what" was one of the astonishment, not the "what" of interrogation. No, it was not. You said "what" in order to humiliate her. What is the purpose of all your harping on petty affectations? Why this continual irritation at the sight of other peoples' stupidities? What of your own stupidities and affectations? Why is it impossible for you to understand, except in terms of art, her action? She killed herself because she was afraid to face her troubles—an abortion or the birth of a bastard. Absurd; she never asked you to marry her. You do not understand.

He crouched over his drink, Tiger Darwin, his eyes half shut—desperate.

I wonder if she was able to avoid generalizing before she killed herself. I am sure it was not trouble, that was uppermost in her mind, but the rag-tag of some "philosophy." Although I did my best to laugh away finita la comedia, I am certain that some such catch-word of disillusion was in her mouth when she turned the trick. She probably decided that Love, Life, Death, all could be contained in an epigram: "The things which are of value in Life are empty and rotten and trifling; Love is but a flitting shadow, a lure, a gimcrack, a kickshaw. And Death?—bah! What, then, is there still detaining you in this vale of tears?" Can it be that the only thing that bothers me in a statement of this sort is the wording? Or is it because there is something arty about suicide? Suicide: Werther, the Cosmic Urge, the Soul, the Quest, and Otto Greenbaum, Phil Beta Kappa, Age seventeen— Life is unworthy of him; and Haldington Knape, Oxford, author, man-about-town, big game hunter—Life is too tiresome; and Terry Kornflower, poet, no hat, shirt open to the navel—Life is too crude; and Janey Davenport, pregnant, unmarried, jumps from a studio window in Paris —Life is too difficult. O. Greenbaum, H. Knape, T. Kornflower, J. Davenport, all would agree that "Life is but the span from womb to tomb; a sigh, a smile; a chill, a fever; a throe of pain, a spasm of volupty: then a gasping for breath, and the comedy is over, the song is ended, ring down the curtain, the clown is dead."

The clown is dead; the curtain is down. And when I say clown, I mean you. After all, aren't we all . . . aren't we all clowns? Of course, I know it's old stuff; but what difference does that make? Life *is* a stage; and *we* are clowns. What is more tragic than the role of clown? What more filled with all the essentials of great art?—pity and irony. Get it? The thousands of sweating, laughing, grimacing, jeering animals out front—you have just set them in the aisles, when in comes a messenger. Your wife has run away with the boarder, your son has killed a man, the baby has cancer. Or maybe you ain't married. Coming from the bathroom, you discover that you have gonorrhoea, or you get a telegram that your mother is dead, or your father, or your sister, or your brother. Now get the picture. Outside, after your turn, the customers are hollering and screaming: "Do your stuff, kid! We want Beagle! Let's have Beagle! He's a wow!" The clowns down front are laughing, whistling, belching, crying, sweating, and eating peanuts. And you—you are back-stage, hiding in the shadow of an old prop. Clutching your bursting head with both hands, you hear nothing but the dull roar of your misfortunes. Slowly there filters through your clenched fingers the cries of your brother clowns. Your first thought is to rush out there and cut your throat before their faces with a last terrific laugh. But soon you are out front again doing your stuff, the same superb Beagle: dancing, laughing, singing—*acting*. Finally the curtain comes down, and, in your dressing room before the mirror, you make the faces that won't come off with the grease paint—the faces you will never make down front.

Beagle ordered another cognac and washed it down with a small beer. The saucers had begun to pile up before him on the table.

Well, Janey's death is a joke. A young, unmarried woman on discovering herself to be pregnant commits suicide. A very old and well-known way out of a very old and stale predicament. The moth and the candle, the fly and the spider, the butterfly and the rain, the clown and the curtain, all could be cited as having prepared one [oh how tediously!] for her suicide.

Another cognac! After this cognac, he would go to the Café Carcas and wait for a friend to bring him news of Janey's death.

How shall I receive the devastating news? In order to arouse no adverse criticism, it will be necessary for me to bear in mind that I come of an English-speaking race and therefore am cold, calm, collected, almost stolid, in the face of calamity. And, as the death is that of a very intimate friend, it is important that I show, in some subtle way, that I am hard hit for all my pretence of coldness. Or perhaps because the Carcas is full of artists, I can refuse to stop dreaming, refuse to leave my ivory tower, refuse to disturb that brooding white bird, my spirit. A wave of the hand: "Yes, really. You don't say so?—quite dead." Or I can play one of my favorite roles, be the "Buffoon of the New Eternities" and cry: "Death, what is it? Life, what is it? Life is of course the absence of Death; and Death merely the absence of Life." But I might get into an argument unbecoming one who is lamenting the loss of a loved one. For the sake of the waiters, I will be a quiet, sober, gentle, umbrella-carrying Mr. B. Darwin, and out of a great sadness sob: "Oh, my darling, why did you do it? Oh why?" Or, best of all, like Hamlet, I will feign madness; for if they discover what lies in my heart they will lynch me.

MESSENGER

"Beagle! Beagle! Janey has fallen from the window and is no more."

PATRONS, WAITERS, ETC., AT THE CAFÉ CARCAS

"The girl you lived with is dead."

"Poor Janey. Poor Beagle. Terrible, terrible death."
"And so young she was, and so beautiful . . . in the cold street she lay."

B. HAMLET DARWIN
"Bromius! Iacchus! Son of Zeus!"

PATRONS, WAITERS, ETC.
"Don't you understand, man? The girl you lived with is dead. Your sweetheart is dead. She has killed herself. She is dead!"

B. HAMLET DARWIN
"Bromius! Iacchus! Son of Zeus!"

PATRONS, WAITERS, ETC.
"He's drunk."
"Greek gods!—does he think we don't know he's a Methodist?"
"This is no time for blasphemy!"
"A little learning goes to the heads of fools."
"Yes, drink deep of the Pierian spring or . . .'"
"Very picturesque though, 'Bromius! Iacchus!' very picturesque."

B. HAMLET DARWIN
" 'O esca vermium! O massa pulveris!' Where is the rich Dives? He who was always eating? He is no longer even eaten."

PATRONS, WAITERS, ETC.
"A riddle! A riddle!"
"He is looking for a friend."
"He has lost something. Tell him to look under the table."

MESSENGER

"He means the worms have eaten Dives; and that, in their turn dead, the worms have been eaten by other worms."

B. HAMLET DARWIN

"Or quick tell me where has gone Samson?—strongest of men. He is no longer even weak. And where, oh tell me, where is the beautiful Appollon? He is no longer even ugly. And where are the snows of yesteryear? And where is Tom Giles? Bill Taylor? Jake Holtz? In other words, 'Here today and gone tomorrow.'"

MESSENGER

"Yes, what he says is but too true. An incident such as the sad demise we are now considering makes one stop 'midst the hustle-bustle of our work-a-day world to ponder the words of the poet who says we are 'nourriture des vers!' Continue, dear brother in sorrow, we attend your every word."

B. HAMLET DARWIN

"I shall begin all over again, folks.

"While I sit laughing with my friends, a messenger stalks into the café. He cries: "Beagle! Beagle! Janey has killed herself!' I jump up, white as a sheet of paper, let us say, and shriek in anguish: 'Bromius! Iacchus! Son of Zeus!' You then demand why I call so loudly on Dionysius. I go into my routine.

"Dionysius! Dionysius! I call on the wine-god because his begetting and birth were so different from Janey's, so different from yours, so different from mine. I call on Dionysius in order to explain the tragedy. A tragedy that is not alone Janey's, but one that is the tragedy of all of us.

"Who among us can boast that he was born three times, as was Dionysius?—once from the womb of 'hapless Semele,' once from the thigh of Zeus, and once from the flames. Or who can say, like Christ, that he was born of a virgin? Or who can even claim to have been born as was Gargantua? Alas! none of us. Yet it is necessary for us to compete—as it was necessary for Janey to compete—with Dionysius the thrice born, Christ son of God, Gargantua born 'midst a torrent of tripe at a most memorable party. You hear the thunder, you see the lightning, you smell the forests, you drink wine—and you attempt to be as was Christ, Dionysius, Gargantua! You who were born from the womb, covered with slime and foul blood, 'midst cries of anguish and suffering.

"At your birth, instead of the Three Kings, the Dove, the Star of Bethlehem, there was only old Doctor Haasenschweitz who wore rubber gloves and carried a towel over his arm like a waiter.

"And how did the lover, your father, come to his beloved? [After a warm day in the office he had seen two dogs in the street.] Did he come in the shape of a swan, a bull, or a shower of gold? No! But with his pants unsupported by braces, came he from the bath-room." . . .

B. Hamlet Darwin towered over his glass of cognac, and, in the theatre of his mind, over a cringing audience —tempestuous, gallant, headstrong, lovable Beagle Dionysius Hamlet Darwin. Up into his giant heart there welled a profound feeling of love for humanity. He choked with emotion as he realized the truth of his observations. Terrible indeed was the competition in which his hearers spent their lives; a competition that demanded their being more than animals.

He raised his hand as though to bless them, and the customers and waiters were silent. Gently, yet with a sense of mighty love, he murmured, "Ah my children." Then, sweeping the Café Carcas with tear-dimmed, eagle's eyes, he cried: "Yet, ah yet, are you expected to compete with Christ whose father is God, with Dionysius whose father is God; you who were Janey Davenport, or one conceived in an offhand manner on a rainy afternoon."

"Cognac! Cognac!"

After building up his tear-jerker routine for a repeat, he blacked out and went into his juggling for the curtain. He climaxed the finale by keeping in the air an Ivory Tower, a Still White Bird, the Holy Grail, the Nails, the Scourge, the Thorns, and a piece of the True Cross.

Yours,

Beagle

"Well, what do you think of them?"

Balso awoke and saw Miss McGeeney, the biographer of Samuel Perkins, sitting beside him at the café table.

"Think of what?"

"The two letters you just read," Miss McGeeney said impatiently. "They form part of a novel I'm writing in the manner of Richardson. Give me your candid opinion: do you think the epistolary style too old-fashioned?"

Refreshed by the nap he had taken, Balso examined his interrogator with interest. She was a fine figure of a woman. He wanted to please her and said:

"A stormy wind blows through your pages, sweeping

the reader breathless . . . witchery and madness. Comparable to George Bernard Shaw. It is a drama of passion that has all the appeal of wild living and the open road. Comparable to George Bernard Shaw. There's magic in its pages, and warm strong sympathy for an alien race."

"Thank you," she said with precision.

How gracious is a woman grateful, thought Balso. He felt young again: the heel of a loaf, a piece of cheese, a bottle of wine and an apple. Clear speakers, naked in the sun. Young students: and the days are very full, and the nights burst with excitement, and life is a torrent roaring.

"Oh!" Balso exclaimed, carried away by these memories of his youth. "Oh!" His mouth formed an O with lips torn angry in laying duck's eggs from a chicken's rectum.

"Oh, what?" Miss McGeeney was obviously annoyed.

"Oh, I loved a girl once. All day she did nothing but place bits of meat on the petals of flowers. She choked the rose with butter and cake crumbs, soiling the crispness of its dainty petals with gravy and cheese. She wanted the rose to attract flies, not butterflies or bees. She wanted to make of her garden a . . ."

"Balso! Balso! Is it you?" cried Miss McGeeney, spilling what was left of his beer, much to the disgust of the waiter who hovered near.

"Balso! Balso! Is it you?" she cried again before he could answer. "Don't you recognize me? I'm Mary. Mary McGeeney, your old sweetheart."

Balso realized that she was indeed Mary. Changed, alas! but with much of the old Mary left, particularly about the eyes. No longer was she dry and stick-like, but a woman, warmly moist.

They sat and devoured each other with looks until the waiter suggested that they leave as he wanted to close the place and go home.

They left arm-in-arm, walking as in a dream. Balso did

the steering and they soon found themselves behind a thick clump of bushes. Miss McGeeney lay down on her back with her hands behind her head and her knees wide apart. Balso stood over her and began a speech the intent of which was obvious.

"First," he said, "let us consider the political aspect. You who talk of Liberty and cling to the protection of Dogma in the face of Life and the Army of Unutterable Physical Law, cast, I say, cast free the anchors, let go the moorings of your desires! Let to the breezes flap the standard of your revolt!

"Also we must consider the philosophical aspects of the proposed act. Nature has lent you for a brief time a few organs capable of giving pleasure. Among these are to be listed the sexual ones. The organs of sex offer in reward for their intelligent use a very intense type of pleasure. Pleasure, it is necessary to admit, is the only good. It is only reasonable to say that if pleasure is desirable—and who besides a few fanatics say it is not?—one should get all the pleasure possible. First it is important to dissociate certain commonplace ideas. As a thinking person, as an individualist—and you are both of these, are you not, love?—it is necessary to dissociate the idea of pleasure from that of generation. Furthermore, it is necessary to disregard one's unreasonable moral training. Sex, not marriage, is a sacrament. You admit it? Then why allow an ancient, inherited code to foist on you, a thinking being, the old, outmoded strictures? Sexual acts are not sins, errors, faults, weaknesses. The sexual acts give pleasure, and pleasure is desirable. So come, Mary, let us have some fun.

"And for the sake of Art, Mary. You desire to write, do you not, love? And you must admit that without knowing what all the shooting is about, a sincere artist is badly handicapped. How can you portray men if you have never known a man? How can you read and understand, see and understand, without ever having known the divine excitement? How can you hope to motivate a theft, a murder, a rape, a suicide, convincingly? And are you ever out of themes? In my bed, love, you will find new themes, new interpretations, new experiences. You will be able to judge for yourself whether love is only three minutes of rapture followed by a feeling of profound disgust, or the all-consuming fire, the divine principle, a foretaste of the joys of heaven? Come, Mary McGeeney, to bed and a new world.

"And now, finally, we come to the Time-argument. Do not confuse what I shall say under this head with the theories so much in vogue among the metaphysicians and physicists, those weavers of the wind. My 'Time' is that of the poets. In a little while, love, you will be dead; that is my burden. In a little while, we all will be dead. Golden lads and chimney-sweeps, all dead. And when dying, will you be able to say, I turn down an empty glass, having drunk to the full, lived to the full? Is it not madness to deny life? Hurry! Hurry! for all is soon over. Blown, O rose! in the morning, thou shalt fade ere noon. Do you realize the tune the clock is playing? The seconds, how they fly! All is soon over! All is soon over! Let us snatch, while yet we may, in this brief span, whose briefness merely gilds the bubble so soon destroyed, some few delights. Have you thought of the grave? O love! have you thought of the grave and of the change that shall come over your fair body? Your most beautiful bride—though now she be pleasant and sweet to the nose—will be damnably mouldy a hundred years hence. O how small a part of time they share, that are so wonderous sweet and fair. Ah, make the most of what we yet may spend before we too into the dust descend. Into the dust, Mary! Thy sweet plenty, in the dust. I tremble, I burn for thy sweet embrace. Be not miserly with thy white flesh. Give your gracious body, for such a short time lent you. Give, for in the giving you shall receive and still have what you give. Only time can rob you of your flesh, I cannot. And time will rob you—it will, it will! And those who husbanded the golden grain, and those who flung it to the wind like rain . . ."

Here Balso threw himself to the ground beside his beloved.

How did she receive him? At first, by saying no.

No. No! Innocent, confused. Oh Balso! Oh Balso! with pictures of the old farm house, old pump, old folks at home, and the old oaken bucket—ivy over all.

Sir! Stamping her tiny foot—imperative, irate. Sir, how dare you, sir! Do you presume? Down, Rover, I say down! The prying thumbs of insolent chauffeurs. The queen chooses. Elizabeth of England, Catherine of Russia, Faustina of Rome.

These two noes graded into two yes-and-noes.

No . . . Oh . . . Oh, no. Eyes aswim with tears. Voice throaty, husky with repressed passion. Oh, how sweet, sweetheart, sweetheart, sweetheart. Oh, I'm melting. My very bones are liquid. I'll swoon if you don't leave me alone. Leave me alone, I'm dizzy. No . . . No! You beast!

No: No, Balso, not tonight. No, not tonight. No! I'm sorry, Balso, but not tonight. Some other time, perhaps yes, but not tonight. Please be a dear, not tonight. Please!

But Balso would not take no for an answer, and he soon obtained the following yeses:

Allowing hot breath to escape from between moist, open lips: eyes upset, murmurs love. Tiger skin on divan. Spanish shawl on grand piano. Altar of Love. Church and Brothel. Odors of Ind and Afric. There's Egypt in your eyes. Rich, opulent love; beautiful, tapestried love; oriental, perfumed love.

Hard-bitten. Casual. Smart. Been there before. I've had policemen. No trace of a feminine whimper. Decidedly revisiting well-known, well-plowed ground. No new trees, wells, or even fences.

Desperate for life. Live! Experience! Live one's own. Your body is an instrument, an organ or a drum. Harmony. Order. Breasts. The apple of my eye, the pear of my abdomen. What is life without love? I burn! I ache! Hurrah!

Moooompitcher yaaaah. Oh I never hoped to know the passion, the sensuality hidden within you—yes, yes. Drag me down into the mire, drag. Yes! And with your hair the lust from my eyes brush. Yes . . . Yes . . . Ooh! Ah!

The miracle was made manifest. The Two became One. The One that is all things and yet no one of them: the priest and the god, the immolation, the sacrificial rite, the libation offered to ancestors, the incantation, the sacrificial egg, the altar, the ego and the alter ego, as well as the father, the child, and the grandfather of the universe, the mystic doctrine, the purification, the syllable "Om," the path, the master, the witness, the receptacle, the Spirit of Public School 186, the last ferry that leaves for Weehawken at seven.

His body broke free of the bard. It took on a life of its own; a life that knew nothing of the poet Balso. Only to death can this release be likened—to the mechanics of decay. After death the body takes command; it performs the manual of disintegration with a marvelous certainty. So now, his body performed the evolutions of love with a like sureness.

In this activity, Home and Duty, Love and Art, were forgotten.

An army moved in his body, an eager army of hurrying sensations. These sensations marched at first methodically and then hysterically, but always with precision. The army of his body commenced a long intricate drill, a long involved ceremony. A ceremony whose ritual unwound and manoeuvred itself with the confidence and training of chemicals acting under the stimulus of a catalytic agent.

His body screamed and shouted as it marched and uncoiled; then, with one heaving shout of triumph, it fell back quiet.

The army that a moment before had been thundering in his body retreated slowly—victorious, relieved.

A defeat for the word.

Relief from pain.

(from pain of sexual frustration)

Legs with 2 view ①. *Art which can't exist without normal sex. desire.*

② *Left with artist with sublimated self draw*

1 9 3 4

A Cool Million

or, The Dismantling of Lemuel Pitkin

"*John D. Rockefeller would give a cool million to have a stomach like yours.*"—OLD SAYING

1

The home of Mrs. Sarah Pitkin, a widow well on in years, was situated on an eminence overlooking the Rat River, near the town of Ottsville in the state of Vermont. It was a humble dwelling much the worse for wear, yet exceedingly dear to her and her only child, Lemuel.

While the house had not been painted for some time, owing to the straitened circumstances of the little family, it still had a great deal of charm. An antique collector, had one chanced to pass it by, would have been greatly interested in its architecture. Having been built about the time of General Stark's campaign against the British, its lines reflected the character of his army, in whose ranks several Pitkins had marched.

One late fall evening, Mrs. Pitkin was sitting quietly in her parlor, when a knock was heard on her humble door.

She kept no servant, and, as usual, answered the knock in person.

"Mr. Slemp!" she said, as she recognized in her caller the wealthy village lawyer.

"Yes, Mrs. Pitkin, I come upon a little matter of business."

"Won't you come in?" said the widow, not forgetting her politeness in her surprise.

"I believe I will trespass on your hospitality for a brief space," said the lawyer blandly. "Are you quite well?"

"Thank you, sir—quite so," said Mrs. Pitkin as she led the way into the sitting room. "Take the rocking chair, Mr. Slemp," she said, pointing to the best chair which the simple room contained.

"You are very kind," said the lawyer, seating himself gingerly in the chair referred to.

"Where is your son, Lemuel?" continued the lawyer.

"He is in school. But it is nearly time for him to be home; he never loiters." And the mother's voice showed something of the pride she felt in her boy.

"Still in school!" exclaimed Mr. Slemp. "Shouldn't he be helping to support you?"

"No," said the widow proudly. "I set great store by learning, as does my son. But you came on business?"

"Ah, yes, Mrs. Pitkin. I fear that the business may be unpleasant for you, but you will remember, I am sure, that I act in this matter as agent for another."

"Unpleasant!" repeated Mrs. Pitkin apprehensively.

"Yes. Mr. Joshua Bird, Squire Bird, has placed in my

hands for foreclosure the mortgage on your house. That is, he will foreclose," he added hastily, "if you fail to raise the necessary monies in three months from now, when the obligation matures."

"How can I hope to pay?" said the widow brokenly. "I thought that Squire Bird would be glad to renew, as we pay him twelve per cent interest."

"I am sorry, Mrs. Pitkin, sincerely sorry, but he has decided not to renew. He wants either his money or the property."

The lawyer took his hat and bowed politely, leaving the widow alone with her tears.

(It might interest the reader to know that I was right in my surmise. An interior decorator, on passing the house, had been greatly struck by its appearance. He had seen Squire Bird about purchasing it, and that is why that worthy had decided to foreclose on Mrs. Pitkin. The name of the cause of this tragedy was Asa Goldstein, his business, "Colonial Exteriors and Interiors." Mr. Goldstein planned to take the house apart and set it up again in the window of his Fifth Avenue shop.)

As Lawyer Slemp was leaving the humble dwelling, he met the widow's son, Lemuel, on the threshold. Through the open door, the boy caught a glimpse of his mother in tears, and said to Mr. Slemp:

"What have you been saying to my mother to make her cry?"

"Stand aside, boy!" exclaimed the lawyer. He pushed Lem with such great force that the poor lad fell off the porch steps into the cellar, the door of which was unfortunately open. By the time Len had extricated himself, Mr. Slemp was well on his way down the road.

Our hero, although only seventeen years old, was a strong, spirited lad and would have followed after the lawyer but for his mother. On hearing her voice, he dropped the ax which he had snatched up and ran into the house to comfort her.

The poor widow told her son all we have recounted and the two of them sat plunged in gloom. No matter how they racked their brains, they could not discover a way to keep the roof over their heads.

In desperation, Lem finally decided to go and see Mr. Nathan Whipple, who was the town's most prominent citizen. Mr. Whipple had once been President of the United States, and was known affectionately from Maine to California as "Shagpoke" Whipple. After four successful years in office, he had beaten his silk hat, so to speak, into a ploughshare and had refused to run a second time, preferring to return to his natal Ottsville and there become a simple citizen again. He spent all his time between his den in the garage and the Rat River National Bank, of which he was president.

Mr. Whipple had often shown his interest in Lem, and the lad felt that he might be willing to help his mother save her home.

2

Shagpoke Whipple lived on the main street of Ottsville in a two-story frame house with a narrow lawn in front and a garage that once had been a chicken house in the rear. Both buildings had a solid, sober look, and, indeed, no one was ever allowed to create disorder within their precincts.

The house served as a place of business as well as a residence; the first floor being devoted to the offices of the bank and the second functioning as the home of the ex-President. On the porch, next to the front door, was a large bronze plate that read:

RAT RIVER NATIONAL BANK
Nathan "Shagpoke" Whipple
PRES.

Some people might object to turning a part of their
dwelling into a bank, especially if, like Mr. Whipple, they
had hobnobbed with crowned heads. But Shagpoke was
not proud, and he was of the saving kind. He had always
saved: from the first time he received a penny at the age
of five, when he had triumphed over the delusive pleasures of an investment in candy, right down to the time he
was elected President of the United States. One of his
favorite adages was "Don't teach your grandmother to suck
eggs." By this he meant that the pleasures of the body are
like grandmothers, once they begin to suck eggs they
never stop until all the eggs (purse) are dry.

As Lem turned up the path to Mr. Whipple's house, the
sun rapidly sank under the horizon. Every evening at this
time, the ex-President lowered the flag that flew over his
garage and made a speech to as many of the town's citi-
zenry as had stopped to watch the ceremony. During the
first year after the great man's return from Washington,
there used to collect quite a crowd, but this had dwindled
until now, as our hero approached the house, there was
but a lone Boy Scout watching the ceremony. This lad
was not present of his own free will, alas, but had been
sent by his father, who was desirous of obtaining a loan
from the bank.

Lem removed his hat and waited in reverence for Mr.
Whipple to finish his speech.

"All hail Old Glory! May you be the joy and pride of the
American heart, alike when your gorgeous folds shall wanton in the summer air and your tattered fragments be
dimly seen through clouds of war! May you ever wave in

honor, hope and profit, in unsullied glory and patriotic fervor, on the dome of the Capitol, on the tented plain, on the wave-rocked topmast and on the roof of this garage!"

With these words, Shagpoke lowered the flag for which so many of our finest have bled and died, and tenderly gathered it up in his arms. The Boy Scout ran off hurriedly. Lem moved forward to greet the orator.

"I would like to have a few words with you, sir," said our hero.

"Certainly," replied Mr. Whipple with native kindness. "I am never too busy to discuss the problems of youth, for the youth of a nation is its only hope. Come into my den," he added.

The room into which Lem followed Mr. Whipple was situated in the back of the garage. It was furnished with extreme simplicity; some boxes, a cracker barrel, two brass spittoons, a hot stove and a picture of Lincoln were all it held.

When our hero had seated himself on one of the boxes, Shagpoke perched on the cracker barrel and put his congress gaiters near the hot stove. He lined up the distance to the nearest spittoon with a measuring gob of spittle and told the lad to begin.

As it will only delay my narrative and serve no good purpose to report how Lem told about his predicament, I will skip to his last sentence.

"And so," concluded our hero, "the only thing that can save my mother's home is for your bank to take over Squire Bird's mortgage."

"I would not help you by lending you money, even if it were possible for me to do so," was the surprising answer Mr. Whipple gave the boy.

"Why not, sir?" asked Lem, unable to hide his great disappointment.

"Because I believe it would be a mistake. You are too young to borrow."

"But what shall I do?" asked Lem in desperation.

"There are still three months left to you before they can sell your house," said Mr. Whipple. "Don't be discouraged. This is the land of opportunity and the world is an oyster."

"But how am I to earn fifteen hundred dollars (for that was the face value of the mortgage) here in such a short time?" asked Lem, who was puzzled by the ex-President's rather cryptic utterances.

"That is for you to discover, but I never said that you should remain in Ottsville. Do as I did, when I was your age. Go out into the world and win your way."

Lem considered this advice for a while. When he spoke again, it was with courage and determination.

"You are right, sir. I'll go off to seek my fortune." Our hero's eyes shone with a light that bespoke a high heart.

"Good," said Mr. Whipple, and he was genuinely glad. "As I said before, the world is an oyster that but waits for hands to open it. Bare hands are best, but have you any money?"

"Something less than a dollar," said Lem sadly.

"It is very little, my young friend, but it might suffice, for you have an honest face and that is more than gold. But I had thirty-five dollars when I left home to make my way, and it would be nice if you had at least as much."

"Yes, it would be nice," agreed Lem.

"Have you any collateral?" asked Mr. Whipple.

"Collateral?" repeated Lem, whose business education was so limited that he did not even know what the word meant.

"Security for a loan," said Mr. Whipple.

"No, sir, I'm afraid not."

"Your mother has a cow, I think?"

"Yes, Old Sue." The boy's face fell as he thought of parting with that faithful servitor.

"I believe that I could lend you twenty-five dollars on her, maybe thirty," said Mr. Whipple.

"But she cost more than a hundred, and besides she supplies us with milk, butter and cheese, the main part of our simple victuals."

"You do not understand," said Mr. Whipple patiently. "Your mother can keep the cow until the note that she will sign comes due in sixty days from now. This new obligation will be an added incentive to spur you on to success."

"But what if I fail?" asked Lem. Not that he was losing heart, be it said, but he was young and wanted encouragement.

Mr. Whipple understood how the lad felt and made an effort to reassure him.

"America," he said with great seriousness, "is the land of opportunity. She takes care of the honest and industrious and never fails them as long as they are both. This is not a matter of opinion, it is one of faith. On the day that Americans stop believing it, on that day will America be lost.

"Let me warn you that you will find in the world a certain few scoffers who will laugh at you and attempt to do you injury. They will tell you that John D. Rockefeller was a thief and that Henry Ford and other great men are also thieves. Do not believe them. The story of Rockefeller and of Ford is the story of every great American, and you should strive to make it your story. Like them, you were born poor and on a farm. Like them, by honesty and industry, you cannot fail to succeed."

It is needless to say that the words of the ex-President encouraged our young hero just as similar ones have heartened the youth of this country ever since it was freed

from the irksome British yoke. He vowed then and there
to go and do as Rockefeller and Ford had done.

Mr. Whipple drew up some papers for the lad's mother
to sign and ushered him out of the den. When he had gone,
the great man turned to the picture of Lincoln that hung
on the wall and silently communed with it.

3

Our hero's way home led through a path that ran along
the Rat River. As he passed a wooded stretch he cut a
stout stick with a thick gnarled top. He was twirling this
club, as a bandmaster does his baton, when he was startled
by a young girl's shriek. Turning his head, he saw a terri-
fied figure pursued by a fierce dog. A moment's glance
showed him that it was Betty Prail, a girl with whom he
was in love in a boyish way.

Betty recognized him at the same moment.

"Oh, save me, Mr. Pitkin!" she exclaimed, clasping her
hands.

"I will," said Lem resolutely.

Armed with the stick he had most fortunately cut, he
rushed between the girl and her pursuer and brought the
knob down with full force on the dog's back. The attention of the furious animal—a large bulldog—was diverted
to his assailant, and with a fierce howl he rushed upon Lem.
But our hero was wary and expected the attack. He
jumped to one side and brought the stick down with great
force on the dog's head. The animal fell, partly stunned,
his quivering tongue protruding from his mouth.

"It won't do to leave him so," thought Lem; "when he
revives he'll be as dangerous as ever."

He dealt the prostrate brute two more blows which
settled its fate. The furious animal would do no more harm.

"Oh, thank you, Mr. Pitkin!" exclaimed Betty, a trace of

color returning to her cheeks. "I was terribly frightened."

"I don't wonder," said Lem. "The brute was certainly ugly."

"How brave you are!" the young lady said in admiration.

"It doesn't take much courage to hit a dog on the head with a stick," said Lem modestly.

"Many boys would have run," she said.

"What, and left you unprotected?" Lem was indignant. "None but a coward would have done that."

"Tom Baxter was walking with me, and he ran away."

"Did he see the dog chasing you?"

"Yes."

"And what did he do?"

"He jumped over a stone wall."

"All I can say is that that isn't my style," said Lem. "Do you see how the dog froths at the mouth? I believe he's mad."

"How fearful!" exclaimed Betty with a shudder. "Did you suspect that before?"

"Yes, when I first saw him."

"And yet you dared to meet him?"

"It was safer than to run," said Lem, making little of the incident. "I wonder whose dog it was?"

"I'll tell you," said a brutal voice.

Turning his head, Lem beheld a stout fellow about three years older than himself, with a face in which the animal seemed to predominate. It was none other than Tom Baxter, the town bully.

"What have you been doing to my dog?" demanded Baxter with a snarl.

Addressed in this tone, Lem thought it unnecessary to throw away politeness on such a brutal customer.

"Killing him," he answered shortly.

"What business have you killing my dog?" demanded the bully with much anger.

"It was your business to keep the brute locked up, where he wouldn't do any harm," said Lem. "Besides, you saw him attack Miss Prail. Why didn't you interfere?"

"I'll flog you within an inch of your life," said Baxter with an oath.

"You'd better not try it," said Lem coolly. "I suppose you think I ought to have let the dog bite Miss Prail."

"He wouldn't have bitten her."

"He would too. He was chasing her with that intention."

"It was only in sport."

"I suppose he was frothing at the mouth only in sport," said Lem. "The dog was mad. You ought to thank me for killing him because he might have bitten you."

"That don't go down," said Baxter coarsely. "It's much too thin."

"It's true," said Betty Prail, speaking for the first time.

"Of course you'll stand up for him," said the butcher boy (for that was Baxter's business), "but that's neither here nor there. I paid five dollars for that dog, and if he don't pay me what I gave, I'll mash him."

"I shall do nothing of the sort," said Lem quietly. "A dog like that ought to be killed, and no one has any right to let him run loose, risking the lives of innocent people. The next time you get five dollars you ought to invest it better."

"Then you won't pay me the money?" cried the bully in a passion. "I'll break your head."

"Come on," said Lem, "I've got something to say about that," and he squared off scientifically.

"Oh, don't fight him, Mr. Pitkin," said Betty, very much distressed. "He is much stronger than you."

"He'll find that out soon enough, I'm thinking," growled Lem's opponent.

That Tom Baxter was not only larger but stronger than our hero was no doubt true. On the other hand he did not know how to use his strength. It was merely undisciplined brute force. If he could have got Lem around the waist the latter would have been at his mercy, but our hero knew that well enough and didn't choose to allow it. He was a pretty fair boxer, and stood on his defense, calm and wary.

When Baxter rushed in, thinking to seize his smaller opponent, he was greeted by two rapid blows in the face, one of which struck him on the nose, the other in the eye, the effect of both being to make his head spin.

"I'll mash you for that," he yelled in a frenzy of rage, but as he rushed in again he never thought to guard his face. The result was a couple of more blows, the other eye and his mouth being assailed this time.

Baxter was astonished. He had expected to "chaw up" Lem at the first onset. Instead of that, there stood Lem cool and unhurt, while he could feel that his nose and mouth were bleeding and both his eyes were rapidly closing.

He stopped short and regarded Lem as well as he could through his injured optics, then surprised our hero by smiling. "Well," he said, shaking his head sheepishly, "you're the better man. I'm a rough customer, I expect, but I know when I'm bested. There's my hand to show that I don't bear malice."

Lem gave his hand in return without fear that there might be craft in the bully's offer of friendship. The former was a fair-dealing lad himself and he thought that everyone was the same. However, no sooner did Baxter have a hold of his hand than he jerked the poor boy into his embrace and squeezed him insensible.

Betty screamed and fainted, so great was her anxiety for Lem. Hearing her scream, Baxter dropped his victim to the ground and walked to where the young lady lay in a dead faint. He stood over her for a few minutes admiring her beauty. His little pig-like eyes shone with bestiality.

4

It is with reluctance that I leave Miss Prail in the lecherous embrace of Tom Baxter to begin a new chapter, but I cannot with propriety continue my narrative beyond the point at which the bully undressed that unfortunate lady.

However, as Miss Prail is the heroine of this romance, I would like to use this opportunity to acquaint you with a little of her past history.

On her twelfth brithday, Betty became an orphan with the simultaneous death of her two parents in a fire which also destroyed what little property might have been left her. In this fire, or rather at it, she also lost something which, like her parents, could never be replaced.

The Prail farm was situated some three miles from Ottsville on a rough dirt road, and the amateur fire company, to whose ministrations all the fires in the district were left, was not very enthusiastic about dragging their apparatus to it. To tell the truth, the Ottsville Fire Company consisted of a set of young men who were more interested in dirty stories, checkers and applejack than they were in fire fighting. When the news of the catastrophe arrived at the fire house, the volunteer firemen were all inebriated, and their chief, Bill Baxter (father to the man in whose arms we left our heroine), was dead drunk.

After many delays, the fire company finally arrived at the Prail farm, but instead of trying to quench the flames they immediately set to work and looted the place.

Betty, although only twelve years old at the time, was a well-formed little girl with the soft, voluptuous lines of a beautiful woman. Dressed only in a cotton nightgown, she was wandering among the firemen begging them to save her parents, when Bill Baxter noticed her budding form and enticed her into the woodshed.

In the morning, she was found lying naked on the
ground by some neighbors and taken into their house. She
had a bad cold, but remembered nothing of what Bill Baxter had done to her. She mourned only the loss of her parents.

After a small collection had been taken up by the
minister to purchase an outfit, she was sent to the county
orphan asylum. There she remained until her fourteenth
year, when she was put out as a maid of all work to the
Slemps, a prominent family of Ottsville, the head of which,
Lawyer Slemp, we already know.

As one can well imagine, all was not beer and skittles in
this household for the poor orphan. If she had been less
beautiful, perhaps things would have gone better for her.
As it was, however, Lawyer Slemp had two ugly daughters and a shrewish wife who were very jealous of their
beautiful servant. They saw to it that she was badly
dressed and that she wore her hair only in the ugliest possible manner. Yet despite these things, and although she
had to wear men's shoes and coarse cotton stockings, our
heroine was a great deal more attractive than the other
women of the household.

Lawyer Slemp was a deacon in the church and a very
stern man. Still, one would think that as a male he would
have less against the poor orphan than his women folks.
But, unfortunately, it did not work out this way. Mr.
Slemp beat Betty regularly and enthusiastically. He had
started these beatings when she first came from the asylum as a little girl, and did not stop them when she became a splendid woman. He beat her twice a week on her
bare behind with his bare hand.

It is a hard thing to say about a deacon, but Lawyer
Slemp got little exercise and he seemed to take a great
deal of pleasure in these bi-weekly workouts. As for Betty,
she soon became inured to his blows and did not mind

them as much as the subtler tortures inflicted on her by Mrs. Slemp and her daughters. Besides, Lawyer Slemp, although he was exceedingly penurious, always gave her a quarter when he had finished beating her.

It was with this weekly fifty cents that Betty hoped to effect her escape from Ottsville. She had already obtained part of an outfit, and was on her way home from town with the first store hat she had ever owned when she met Tom Baxter and his dog.

The result of this unfortunate encounter we already know.

5

When our hero regained consciousness, he found himself in a ditch alongside the path on which he had his set-to with Tom Baxter. It had grown quite dark, and he failed to notice Betty in some bushes on the other side of the path. He thought that she must have got safely away.

As he walked home his head cleared and he soon recovered his naturally high spirits. He forgot his unfortunate encounter with the bully and thought only of his coming departure for New York City.

He was greeted at the door of his humble home by his fond parent, who had been waiting anxiously for his return.

"Lem, Lem," said Mrs. Pitkin, "where have you been?"

Although our hero was loth to lie, he did not want to worry his mother unduly, so he said, "Mr. Whipple kept me."

The lad then told her what the ex-President had said. She was quite happy for her son and willingly signed the note for thirty dollars. Like all mothers, Mrs. Pitkin was certain that her child must succeed.

Bright and early the next morning, Lem took the note

to Mr. Whipple and received thirty dollars minus twelve per cent interest in advance. He then bought a ticket for New York at the local depot, and waited there for the arrival of the steam cars.

Our hero was studying the fleeting scenery of New England when he heard someone address him.

"Papers, magazines, all the popular novels! Something to read, mister?"

It was the news butcher, a young boy with an honest, open countenance.

Our hero was eager to talk, so he spoke to the newsboy.

"I'm not a great one for reading novels," he said. "My Aunt Nancy gave my ma one once but I didn't find much in it. I like facts and I like to study, though."

"I ain't much on story reading either," said the news butcher. "Where are you goin' ?"

"To New York to make my fortune," said Lem candidly.

"Well, if you can't make money in New York, you can't make money anywhere." With this observation he began to hawk his reading matter farther down the aisle.

Lem again took up his study of the fleeting scenery. This time he was interrupted by a stylishly dressed young man who came forward and accosted him.

"Is this seat engaged?" the stranger asked.

"Not as I know of?" replied Lem with a friendly smile.

"Then with your kind permission I will occupy it," said the over-dressed stranger.

"Why, of course," said our hero.

"You are from the country, I presume," he continued affably as he sank into the seat alongside our hero.

"Yes, I am. I live near Bennington in the town of Ottsville. Were you ever there?"

"No. I suppose you are taking a vacation trip to the big city?"

"Oh, no; I'm leaving home to make my fortune."

"That's nice. I hope you are successful. By the way, the Mayor of New York is my uncle."

"My, is that so?" said Lem with awe.

"Yes indeed, my name is Wellington Mape."

"Glad to make your acquaintance, Mr. Mape. I'm Lemuel Pitkin."

"Indeed! An aunt of mine married a Pitkin. Perhaps we're related."

Lem was quite elated at the thought that he might be kin to the Mayor of New York without knowing it. He decided that his new acquaintance must be rich because of his clothing and his extreme politeness.

"Are you in business, Mr. Mape?" he asked.

"Well, ahem!" was that suave individual's rejoinder. "I'm afraid I'm rather an idler. My father left me a cool million, so I don't feel the need of working."

"A cool million!" ejaculated Lem. "Why, that's ten times a hundred thousand dollars."

"Just so," said Mr. Mape, smiling at the lad's enthusiasm.

"That's an awful pile of money! I'd be satisfied if I had five thousand right now."

"I'm afraid that five thousand wouldn't last me very long," said Mr. Mape with an amused smile.

"Gee! Where would anybody get such a pile of money unless they inherited it?"

"That's easy," said the stranger. "Why, I've made as much in one day in Wall Street."

"You don't say."

"Yes, I do say. You can take my word for it."

"I wish I could make some money," said Lem wistfully, as he thought of the mortgage on his home.

"A man must have money to make money. If now, you had some money . . ."

"I've got a little under thirty dollars," said Lem.

"Is that all?"

"Yes, that's all. I had to give Mr. Whipple a note to borrow it."

"If that's all the money you have, you'd better take good care of it. I regret to say that despite the efforts of the Mayor, my uncle, there are still many crooks in New York."

"I intend to be careful."

"Then you keep your money in a safe place?"

"I haven't hidden it because a secret pocket is the first place a thief would look. I keep it loose in my trousers where nobody would think I carried so much money."

"You are right. I can see that you are a man of the world."

"Oh, I can take care of myself, I guess," said Lem with the confidence of youth.

"That comes of being a Pitkin. I'm glad to know that we're related. You must call on me in New York."

"Where do you live?"

"At the Ritz. Just ask for Mr. Wellington Mape's suite of rooms."

"Is it a good place to live?"

"Why, yes. I pay three dollars a day for my board, and the incidentals carry my expenses up to as high as forty dollars a week."

"Gee," ejaculated Lem. "I could never afford it—that is, at first." And our hero laughed with the incurable optimism of youth.

"You of course should find a boarding house where they give you plain but solid fare for a reasonable sum. . . . But I must bid you good morning, a friend is waiting for me in the next car."

After the affable Mr. Wellington Mape had taken his departure, Lem turned again to his vigil at the car window.

The news butcher had changed his cap. "Apples, bananas, oranges!" he shouted as he came down the aisle with a basket of fruit on his arm.

Lem stopped his rapid progress to ask him the price of an orange. It was two cents, and he decided to buy one to eat with the hard-boiled egg his mother had given him. But when our hero thrust his hand into his pocket, a wild spasm contracted his features. He explored further, with growing trepidation, and a sickly pallor began to spread over his face.

"What's the matter?" asked Steve, for that was the train boy's name.

"I've been robbed! My money's gone! All the money Mr. Whipple lent me has been stolen!"

6

"I wonder who did it?" asked Steve.

"I can't imagine," answered Lem brokenly.

"Did they get much?"

"All I had in the world. . . . A little less than thirty dollars."

"Some smart leather must have gotten it."

"Leather?" queried our hero, not understanding the argot of the underworld with which the train boy was familiar.

"Yes, leather—pickpocket. Did anybody talk to you on the train?"

"Only Mr. Wellington Mape, a rich young man. He is kin to the Mayor of New York."

"Who told you that?"

"He did himself."

"How was he dressed?" asked Steve, whose suspicions were aroused. (He had been "wire"—scout—to a "leather" when small and knew all about the dodge.) "Did he wear a pale blue hat?"

"Yes."

"And looked a great swell?"

"Yes."

"He got off at the last station and your dough-re-me went with him."

"You mean he got my money? Well, I never. He told me he was worth a cool million and boarded at the Ritz Hotel."

"That's the way they all talk—big. Did you tell him where you kept your money?"

"Yes, I did. But can't I get it back?"

"I don't see how. He got off the train."

"I'd like to catch hold of him," said Lem, who was very angry.

"Oh, he'd hit you with a piece of lead pipe. But look through your pockets, maybe he left you a dollar."

Lem put his hand into the pocket in which he had carried his money and drew it out as though he had been bitten. Between his fingers he held a diamond ring.

"What's that?" asked Steve.

"I don't know," said Lem with surprise. "I don't think I ever saw it before. Yes, by gum, I did. It must have dropped off the crook's finger when he picked my pocket. I saw him wearing it."

"Boy!" exclaimed the train boy. "You're sure in luck. Talk about falling in a privy and coming up with a gold watch. You're certainly it. With a double t."

"What is it worth?" asked Lem eagerly.

"Permit me to look at it, my young friend, perhaps I can tell you," said a gentleman in a gray derby hat, who was sitting across the aisle. This stranger had been listening with great curiosity to the dialogue between our hero and the train boy.

"I am a pawnbroker," he said. "If you let me examine the ring, I can surely give you some idea of its value."

Lem handed the article in question to the stranger, who put a magnifying glass into his eye and looked at it carefully.

"My young friend, that ring is worth all of fifty dollars," he announced.

"I'm certainly in luck," said Lem. "The crook only stole twenty-eight dollars and sixty cents from me. But I'd rather have my money back. I don't want any of his."

"I'll tell you what I'll do," said the self-styled pawnbroker. "I'll advance you twenty-eight dollars and sixty cents against the ring, and agree to give it back for that sum and suitable interest if the owner should ever call for it."

"That's fair enough," said Lem gratefully, and he pocketed the money that the stranger tendered him.

Our hero paid for the piece of fruit that he had bought from the train boy and ate it with quiet contentment. In the meantime, the "pawnbroker" prepared to get off the train. When he had gathered together his meager luggage, he shook hands with Lem and gave him a receipt for the ring.

But no sooner had the stranger left than a squad of policemen armed with sawed-off shotguns entered and started down the aisle. Lem watched their progress with great interest. His interest, however, changed to alarm when they stopped at his seat and one of them caught him roughly by the throat. Handcuffs were then snapped around his wrists. Weapons pointed at his head.

7

"Begorra, we've got him," said Sergeant Clancy, who was in charge of the police squad.

"But I haven't done anything," expostulated Lem, turning pale.

"None of your lip, sweetheart," said the sergeant. "Will

you go quietly or will you go quietly?" Before the poor
lad had a chance to express his willingness to go, the police officer struck him an extremely hard blow on the head
with his club.

Lem slumped down in his seat and Sergeant Clancy
ordered his men to carry the boy off the train. A patrol
wagon was waiting at the depot. Lem's unconscious form
was dumped into the "Black Maria" and the police drove
to the station house.

When our hero regained consciousness some hours later,
he was lying on the stone floor of a cell. The room was full
of detectives and the air was foul with cigar smoke. Lem
opened one eye, unwittingly giving the signal for the detectives to go into action.

"'Fess up," said Detective Grogan, but before the boy
could speak he kicked him in the stomach with his heavy
boot.

"Faith now," interfered Detective Reynolds, "give the
lad a chance." He bent over Lem's prostrate form with a
kind smile on his face and said, "Me lad, the jig is up."

"I'm innocent," protested Lem. "I didn't do anything."

"You stole a diamond ring and sold it," said another detective.

"I did not," replied Lem, with as much fire as he could
muster under the circumstances. "A pickpocket dropped
it in my pocket and I pawned it with a stranger for thirty
dollars."

"Thirty dollars!" exclaimed Detective Reynolds, his voice
giving great evidence of disbelief. "Thirty dollars for a
ring that cost more than a thousand. Me lad, it won't
wash." So saying the detective drew back his foot and
kicked poor Lem behind the ear even harder than his col-
league had done.

Our hero lost consciousness again, as was to be expected, and the detectives left his cell, having first made sure that he was still alive.

A few days later, Lem was brought to trial, but neither judge nor jury would believe his story.

Unfortunately, Stamford, the town in which he had been arrested, was in the midst of a crime wave and both the police and the judiciary were anxious to send people to jail. It also counted heavily against him that the man who had posed as a pawnbroker on the train was in reality Hiram Glazer, alias "The Pinhead," a notorius underworld character. This criminal turned state's evidence and blamed the crime on our hero in return for a small fee from the district attorney, who was shortly coming up for re-election.

Once the verdict of guilty had been brought in, Lem was treated with great kindness by everyone, even by the detectives who had been so brutal in the station house. It was through their recommendations, based on what they called his willingness to cooperate, that he received only fifteen years in the penitentiary.

Our hero was immediately transferred to prison, where he was incarcerated exactly five weeks after his departure from Ottsville. It would be hard to say from this that justice is not swift, although, knowing the truth, we must add that it is not always sure.

The warden of the state prison, Ezekiel Purdy, was a kind man if stern. He invariably made all newcomers a little speech of welcome and greeted Lem with the following words:

"My son, the way of the transgressor is hard, but at your age it is still possible to turn from it. However, do not squirm, for you will get no sermon from me."

(Lem was not squirming. The warden's expression was purely rhetorical.)

"Sit down for a moment," added Mr. Purdy, indicating the chair in which he wanted Lem to sit. "Your new duties can wait yet awhile, as can the prison barber and tailor."

The warden leaned back in his chair and sucked meditatively on his enormous calabash pipe. When he began to talk again, it was with ardor and conviction.

"The first thing to do is to draw all your teeth," he said. "Teeth are often a source of infection and it pays to be on the safe side. At the same time we will begin a series of cold showers. Cold water is an excellent cure for morbidity."

"But I am innocent," cried Lem, when the full significance of what the warden had said dawned on him. "I am not morbid and I never had a toothache in my life."

Mr. Purdy dismissed the poor lad's protests with an airy wave of his hand. "In my eyes," he said, "the sick are never guilty. You are merely sick, as are all criminals. And as for your other argument; please remember that an ounce of prevention is worth a ton of cure. Because you have never had a toothache does not mean that you will never have one."

Lem could not help but groan.

"Be of good cheer, my son," said the warden brightly, as he pressed a button on his desk to summon a guard.

A few minutes later our hero was led off to the prison dentist, where we will not follow him just yet.

8

Several chapters back I left our heroine, Betty Prail, lying naked under a bush. She was not quite so fortunate as Lem, and did not regain consciousness until after he had returned home.

When she recovered the full possession of her faculties, she found herself in what she thought was a large box that was being roughly shaken by some unknown agency. In a little while, however, she realized that she was in reality lying on the bottom of a wagon.

"Could it be that she was dead?" she asked herself. But no, she heard voices, and besides she was still naked. "No matter how poor a person is," she comforted herself, "they wrap him or her up in something before burial."

There were evidently two men on the driver's seat of the wagon. She tried to understand what they were saying, but could not because they spoke a foreign tongue. She was able to recognize their language as Italian, however, having had some few music lessons in the orphan asylum.

"Gli diede uno scudo, il che lo rese subito gentile," said one of her captors to the other in a guttural voice.

"Si, si," affirmed the other. "Questa vita terrena e quasi un prato, che'l serpente tra fiori giace." After this bit of homely philosophy, they both lapsed into silence.

But I do not want to mystify my readers any longer. The truth was that the poor girl had been found by white slavers, and was being taken to a house of ill fame in New York City.

The trip was an exceedingly rough one for our heroine. The wagon in which she was conveyed had no springs to speak of, and her two captors made her serve a severe apprenticeship to the profession they planned for her to follow.

Late one night, the Italians halted their vehicle before the door of a Chinese laundry somewhere near Mott Street. After descending from their dilapidated conveyance, they scanned the street both up and down for a possible policeman. When they had made sure that it was deserted, they covered their captive with some old sacking and bundled her into the laundry.

There they were greeted by an ancient Chinaman, who

was doing sums on an abacus. This son of the Celestial
Empire was a graduate of the Yale University in Shanghai,
and he spoke Italian perfectly.

"Qualche cosa de nuovo, signori?" he asked.

"Molto, molto," said the older and more villainous looking of the two foreigners. "La vostra lettera l'abbiamo
ricevuto, ma il danaro no," he added with a shrewd smile.

"Queste sette medaglie le trovero, compaesano," answered the Chinaman in the same language.

After this rather cryptic dialogue, the Chinaman led
Betty through a secret door into a sort of reception room.
This chamber was furnished in luxurious oriental splendor.
The walls were sheathed in a pink satin that had been
embroidered with herons in silver by some cunning work-
man. On the floor was a silk rug that must have cost more
than a thousand dollars, the colors of which could well
vie with the rainbow. Before a hideous idol, incense was
burning, and its heady odor filled the air. It was evident
that neither pains nor expense had been spared in the
decoration of the room.

The old Chinaman struck a gong, and ere its musical
note died away an oriental woman with bound feet came
to lead Betty off.

When she had gone, Wu Fong, for that was the Chinaman's name, began to haggle with the two Italians over
her purchase price. The bargaining was done in Italian,
and rather than attempt to make a word-for-word report
of the transaction I shall give only the result. Betty was
knocked down to the Chinaman for six hundred dollars.

This was a big price, so far as prices went in the white
slave market. But Wu Fong was set on having her. In
fact it was he who had sent the two to scour the New England countryside for a real American girl. Betty suited him
down to the ground.

The reader may be curious to know why he wanted an

American girl so badly. Let me say now that Wu Fong's establishment was no ordinary house of ill fame. It was like that more famous one in the Rue Chabanis, Paris, France—a "House of All Nations." In his institution he already had a girl from every country in the known world except ours, and now Betty rounded out the collection.

Wu Fong was confident that he would soon have his six hundred dollars back with interest, for many of his clients were from non-Aryan countries and would appreciate the services of a genuine American. Apropos of this, it is lamentable but a fact, nevertheless, that the inferior races greatly desire the women of their superiors. This is why the Negroes rape so many white women in our southern states.

Each one of the female inmates of Wu Fong's establishment had a tiny two-room suite for her own use, furnished and decorated in the style of the country from which she came. Thus, Marie, the French girl, had an apartment that was Directoire. Celeste's rooms (there were two French girls because of their traditional popularity) were Louis the Fourteenth; she being the fatter of the two.

In her suite, the girl from Spain, Conchita, had a grand piano with a fancy shawl gracefully draped over it. Her arm-chair was upholstered in horsehide fastened by large buttons, and it had enormous steer horns for arms. On one of her walls a tiny balcony had been painted by a poor but consummate artist.

There is little use in my listing the equipment of the remaining some fifty-odd apartments. Suffice it to say that the same idea was carried out with excellent taste and real historical knowledge in all of them.

Still wearing the sacking into which the Italians had bundled her, our heroine was led to the apartment that had been prepared against her arrival.

The proprietor of the house had hired Asa Goldstein to

decorate this suite and it was a perfect colonial interior. Antimacassars, ships in bottles, carved whalebone, hooked rugs—all were there. It was Mr. Goldstein's boast that even Governor Windsor himself could not have found anything wrong with the design or furnishings.

Betty was exhausted, and immediately fell asleep on the poster bed with its candlewick spread. When she awoke, she was given a hot bath, which greatly refreshed her. She was then dressed by two skillful maids.

The costume that she was made to wear had been especially designed to go with her surroundings. While not exactly in period, it was very striking, and I will describe it as best I can for the benefit of my feminine readers.

The dress had a full waist made with a yoke and belt, a gored skirt, long, but not too long to afford a very distinct view of a well-turned ankle and a small, shapely foot encased in a snowy cotton stocking and a low-heeled black slipper. The material of the dress was chintz—white ground with a tiny brown figure—finished at the neck with a wide white ruffle. On her hands she was made to wear black silk mitts with half-fingers. Her hair was worn in a little knot on the top of her head, and one thick short curl was kept in place by a puff-comb on each side of her face.

Breakfast, for so much time had elapsed, was served her by an old Negro in livery. It consisted of buckwheat cakes with maple syrup, Rhode Island Johnny cakes, bacon biscuits, and a large slice of apple pie.

(Wu Fong was a great stickler for detail, and, like many another man, if he had expended as much energy and thought honestly he would have made even more money without having to carry the stigma of being a brothel-keeper. Alas!)

So resilient are the spirits of the young that Betty did the breakfast full justice. She even ordered a second helping of pie, which was brought to her at once by the darky.

After Betty had finished eating, she was given some embroidery to do. With the reader's kind permission we will leave her while she is still sewing, and before the arrival of her first client, a pockmarked Armenian rug merchant from Malta.

9

Justice will out. I am happy to acquaint my readers with the fact that the real criminal, Mr. Wellington Mape, was apprehended by the police some weeks after Lem had been incarcerated in the state penitentiary.

But our hero was in a sorry state when the Governor's pardon arrived, and for a while it looked as though the reprieve had come too late. The poor lad was in the prison infirmary with a bad case of pneumonia. Weakened greatly by the drawing of all his teeth, he had caught cold after the thirteenth icy shower and the fourteenth had damaged his lungs.

Due to his strong physique, however, and a constitution that had never been undermined by the use of either tobacco or alcohol, Lem succeeded in passing the crisis of the dread pulmonary disease.

On the first day that his vision was normal, he was surprised to see Shagpoke Whipple go through the prison infirmary carrying what was evidently a bedpan and dressed in the uniform of a convict.

"Mr. Whipple," Lem called. "Mr. Whipple."

The ex-President turned and came towards the boy's bed.

"Hello, Lem," said Shagpoke, putting down the utensil he was carrying. "I'm glad to see that you're better."

"Thank you, sir. But what are you doing here?" asked Lem with bewildered surprise.

"I'm the trusty in charge of this ward. But what you really mean, I take it, is why am I here?"

The elderly statesman looked around. He saw that the guard was busy talking to a pretty nurse and drew up a chair.

"It's a long story," said Mr. Whipple with a sigh. "But the long and short of it is that the Rat River National failed and its depositors sent me here."

"That's too bad, sir," Lem said sympathetically. "And after all you had done for the town."

"Such is the gratitude of the mob, but in a way I can't blame them," Mr. Whipple said with all the horse sense for which he was famous. "Rather do I blame Wall Street and the Jewish international bankers. They loaded me up with a lot of European and South American bonds, then they forced me to the wall. It was Wall Street working hand in hand with the Communists that caused my downfall. The bankers broke me, and the Communists circulated lying rumors about my bank in Doc Slack's barber shop. I was the victim of an un-American conspiracy."

Mr. Whipple sighed again, then said in a militant tone of voice: "My boy, when we get out of here, there are two evils undermining this country which we must fight with tooth and nail. These two archenemies of the American Spirit, the spirit of fair play and open competition, are Wall Street and the Communists."

"But how is my mother?" interrupted Lem, "and whatever became of our house? And the cow—did you have to sell her?" Our hero's voice trembled as he asked these questions, for he feared the worst.

"Alas," sighed Mr. Whipple, "Squire Bird foreclosed his mortgage and Asa Goldstein took your home to his store in New York City. There is some talk of his selling it to the Metropolitan Museum. As for the cow, the creditors of my bank sheriffed her. Your mother disappeared. She wandered off during the foreclosure sale, and neither hair nor hide of her was seen again."

This terrible intelligence made our hero literally groan with anguish.

In an effort to cheer the boy up, Mr. Whipple kept on talking. "Your cow taught me a lesson," he said. "She was about the only collateral I had that paid one hundred cents on the dollar. The European bonds didn't bring ten cents on the dollar. The next bank I own will mortgage nothing but cows, good American cows."

"You expect to keep a bank again?" asked Lem, making a brave attempt not to think of his own troubles.

"Why, certainly," replied Shagpoke. "My friends will have me out of here shortly. Then I will run for political office, and after I have shown the American people that Shagpoke is still Shagpoke, I will retire from politics and open another bank. In fact, I am even considering opening the Rat River National a second time. I should be able to buy it in for a few cents on the dollar."

"Do you really think you can do it?" asked our hero with wonder and admiration.

"Why, of course I can," answered Mr. Whipple. "I am an American businessman, and this place is just an incident in my career. My boy, I believe I once told you that you had an almost certain chance to succeed because you were born poor and on a farm. Let me now tell you that your chance is even better because you have been in prison."

"But what am I to do when I get out?" asked Lem with ill-concealed desperation.

"Be an inventor," Mr. Whipple replied without a moment's hesitation. "The American mind is noted for its ingenuity. All the devices of the modern world, from the safety pin to four-wheel brakes, were invented by us."

"But I don't know what to invent," said Lem.

"That's easy. Before you leave here I will give you several of my inventions to work on. If you perfect them we will split fifty-fifty."

"That'll be great!" exclaimed Lem with increased cheerfulness.

"My young friend, you don't want me to think that you were in any way discouraged by the misfortunes that befell you?" asked Mr. Whipple with simulated surprise.

"But I didn't even get to New York," apologized Lem.

"America is still a young country," Mr. Whipple said, assuming his public manner, "and like all young countries, it is rough and unsettled. Here a man is a millionaire one day and a pauper the next, but no one thinks the worse of him. The wheel will turn, for that is the nature of wheels. Don't believe the fools who tell you that the poor man hasn't got a chance to get rich any more because the country is full of chain stores. Office boys still marry their employers' daughters. Shipping clerks are still becoming presidents of railroads. Why, only the other day, I read where an elevator operator won a hundred thousand dollars in a sweepstake and was made a partner in a brokerage house. Despite the Communists and their vile propaganda against individualism, this is still the golden land of opportunity. Oil wells are still found in people's back yards. There are still gold mines hidden away in our mountain fastnesses. America is . . ."

But while Shagpoke was still speaking, a prison guard came by and forced him hurriedly to resume his duties. He left with his bedpan before Lem had an opportunity to thank him properly for his inspiring little talk.

Helped not a little by the encouragement Mr. Whipple had given him, our hero mended rapidly. One day he was summoned to the office of Mr. Purdy, the warden. That official showed him the pardon from the Governor.

As a parting gift, he presented Lem with a set of false teeth. He then conducted him to the prison gates, and stood there awhile with the boy, for he had grown fond of him.

Shaking Lem's hand in a hearty farewell, Mr. Purdy said:

"Suppose you had obtained a job in New York City that paid fifteen dollars a week. You were here with us in all twenty weeks, so you lost the use of three hundred dollars. However, you paid no board while you were here, which was a saving for you of about seven dollars a week or one hundred and forty dollars. This leaves you the loser by one hundred and sixty dollars. But it would have cost you at least two hundred dollars to have all your teeth extracted, so you're really ahead of the game forty dollars. Also, the set of false teeth I gave you cost twenty dollars new and is worth at least fifteen dollars in its present condition. This makes your profit about fifty-five dollars. Not at all a bad sum for a lad of your age to save in twenty weeks."

10

Along with his civilian clothes, the prison authorities turned back to Lem an envelope containing the thirty dollars he had had in his pockets on the day he was arrested.

He did not loiter in Stamford, but went immediately to the depot and bought a ticket for New York City. When the cars pulled into the station, he boarded them determined not to speak to any strangers. He was helped in this by the fact that he was not as yet used to his false teeth. Unless he exercised great care, they fell into his lap every time he opened his mouth.

He arrived in the Grand Central Station all intact. At first he was quite confused by the hustle and bustle of the

great city, but when a Jehu standing by a broken-down
Pierce Arrow hack accosted him, he had the presence of
mind to shake his head in the negative.

The cabby was a persistent fellow. "Where do you want
to go, young master?" he asked with sneering servility. "Is
it the Ritz Hotel you're looking for?"

Lem took a firm purchase on his store teeth and asked,
"That's one of those high-priced taverns, isn't it?"

"Yes, but I'll take you to a cheap one if you'll hire me."

"What's your charge?"

"Three dollars and a half, and half a dollar for your baggage."

"This is all the baggage I have," said Lem, indicating his
few things tied in a red cotton handkerchief.

"I'll take you for three dollars, then," said the driver with
a superior smile.

"No, thanks, I'll walk," said our hero. "I can't afford to
pay your charge."

"You can't walk; it's over ten miles from this station to
town," replied the Jehu without blushing, although it was
evident that they were at that moment standing almost
directly in the center of the city.

Without another word, Lem turned on his heel and
walked away from the cab driver. As he made his way
through the crowded streets, he congratulated himself on
how he had handled his first encounter. By keeping his
wits about him, he had saved over a tenth of his capital.

Lem saw a peanut stand, and as a matter of policy purchased a bag of the toothsome earth nuts.

"I'm from the country," he said to the honest-appearing
merchant. "Can you direct me to a cheap hotel?"

"Yes," said the sidewalk vendor, smiling at the boy's
candor. "I know of one where they charge only a dollar a
day."

"Is that cheap?" asked our hero in surprise. "What then do they charge at the Ritz?"

"I have never stayed there, but I understand that it is as much as three dollars a day."

"Phew!" whistled Lem. "Think of that now. Twenty-one dollars a week. But I suppose they do you awfully well."

"Yes, I hear they set a very good table."

"Will you be so kind as to direct me to the cheap one of which you first spoke?"

"Certainly."

It was the Commercial House to which the peanut dealer advised Lem to go. This hostelry was located in a down-town street very near the Bowery and was not a stylish inn by any manner of means. However, it was held in good repute by many merchants in a small way of business. Our hero was well satisfied with the establishment when he found it. He had never before seen a fine hotel, and this structure being five stories above the offices seemed to him rather imposing than otherwise.

After being taken to his room, Lem went downstairs and found that dinner was ready, it being just noon. He ate with a country boy's appetite. It was not a luxurious meal, but compared with the table that Warden Purdy set it was a feast for the gods.

When he had finished eating, Lem asked the hotel clerk how to get to Asa Goldstein's store on Fifth Avenue. He was told to walk to Washington Square, then take the bus uptown.

After an exciting ride along the beautiful thoroughfare, Lem descended from the bus before a store, across the front of which was a sign reading

ASA GOLDSTEIN, LTD.
Colonial Exteriors and Interiors

and in the window of which his old home actually stood.

At first the poor boy could not believe his eyes, but, yes, there it was exactly as in Vermont. One of the things that struck him was the seediness of the old house. When he and his mother had lived in it, they had kept it in a much better state of repair.

Our hero stood gazing at the exhibit for so long that he attracted the attention of one of the clerks. This suave individual came out to the street and addressed Lem.

"You admire the architecture of New England?" he said, feeling our hero out.

"No; it's that particular house that interests me, sir," replied Lem truthfully. "I used to live in it. In fact I was born in that very house."

"My, this is interesting," said the clerk politely. "Perhaps you would like to enter the shop and inspect it at firsthand."

"Thank you," replied Lem gratefully. "It would give me a great deal of pleasure so to do."

Our hero followed after the affable clerk and was permitted to examine his old home at close range. To tell the truth, he saw it through a veil of tears, for he could think of nothing but his poor mother who had disappeared.

"I wonder if you would be so kind as to furnish me with a little information?" asked the clerk, pointing to a patched old chest of drawers. "Where would your mother have put such a piece of furniture had she owned it?"

Lem's first thought on inspecting the article in question was to say that she would have kept it in the woodshed, but he thought better of this when he saw how highly the clerk valued it. After a little thought, he pointed to a space next to the fireplace and said, "I think she would have set it there."

"What did I tell you!" exclaimed the delighted clerk to

his colleagues, who had gathered around to hear Lem's answer. "That's just the spot I picked for it."

The clerk then ushered Lem to the door, slipping a two-dollar note into the boy's hand as he shook it good-by. Lem did not want to take the money because he felt that he had not earned it, but he was finally prevailed upon to accept it. The clerk told Lem that he had saved them the fee an expert would have demanded, since it was very important for them to know exactly where the chest of drawers belonged.

Our hero was considerably elated at his stroke of luck and marveled at the ease with which two dollars could be earned in New York. At this rate of pay, he calculated, he would earn ninety-six dollars for an eight-hour day or five hundred and seventy-six dollars for a six-day week. If he could keep it up, he would have a million in no time.

From the store, Lem walked west to Central Park, where he sat down on a bench in the mall near the bridle path to watch the society people ride by on their beautiful horses. His attention was particularly attracted by a man driving a small spring wagon, underneath which ran two fine Dalmatians or coach dogs, as they are sometimes called. Although Lem was unaware of this fact, the man in the wagon was none other than Mr. Asa Goldstein, whose shop he had just visited.

The country-bred boy soon noticed that Mr. Goldstein was not much of a horseman. However, that individual was not driving his beautiful team of matched bays for pleasure, as one might be led to think, but for profit. He had accumulated a large collection of old wagons in his warehouse and by driving one of them in the mall he hoped to start a vogue for that type of equipage and thus sell off his stock.

While Lem was watching the storekeeper's awkward handling of the "leathers" or reins, the off horse, which was very skittish, took fright at a passing policeman and bolted. His panic soon spread to the other horse and the wagon went careening down the path wreaking havoc at every bound. Mr. Goldstein fell out when his vehicle turned over, and Lem had to laugh at the comical expression of mingled disgust and chagrin that appeared on his countenance.

But suddenly Lem's smile disappeared and his jaw became set, for he saw that a catastrophe was bound to occur unless something was immediately done to halt the maddened thoroughbreds.

11

The reason for the sudden disappearance of the smile from our hero's face is easily explained. He had spied an old gentleman and his beautiful young daughter about to cross the bridle path, and saw that in a few more seconds they would be trampled under the iron hooves of the flying beasts.

Lem hesitated only long enough to take a firm purchase on his store teeth, then dashed into the path of the horses. With great strength and agility, he grasped their bridles and dragged them to a rearing halt, a few feet from the astounded and thoroughly frightened pair.

"That lad has saved your lives," said a bystander to the old gentleman, who was none other than Mr. Levi Underdown, president of the Underdown National Bank and Trust Company.

Unfortunately, however, Mr. Underdown was slightly deaf, and, although exceedingly kind, as his many large charities showed, he was very short tempered. He entirely misunderstood the nature of our hero's efforts and thought that the poor boy was a careless groom who had let his charges get out of hand. He became extremely angry.

"I've a mind to give you in charge, young man," said the banker, shaking his umbrella at our hero.

"Oh, don't, father!" interfered his daughter Alice, who also misunderstood the incident. "Don't have him arrested. He was probably paying court to some pretty nursemaid and forgot about his horses." From this we can readily see that the young lady was of a romantic turn of mind.

She smiled kindly at our hero, and led her irate parent from the scene.

Lem had been unable to utter one word in explanation because, during his tussle with the horses, his teeth had jarred loose and without them he was afraid to speak. All he could do was to gaze after their departing backs with mute but ineffectual anguish.

There being nothing else for it, Lem gave over the reins of the team to Mr. Goldstein's groom, who came running up at this juncture, and turned to search for his oral equipment in the mud of the bridle path. While he was thus occupied, a man representing the insurance company with which Mr. Goldstein carried a public liability policy approached him.

"Here is ten dollars, my lad," said the claim adjuster. "The gentleman whose horses you so bravely stopped wishes you to have this money as a reward."

Lem took it without thinking.

"Please sign this for me," added the insurance man, holding out a legal form which released his company from any and all claim to damages.

One of Lem's eyes had been so badly injured by a flying stone that he could not see out of it, but nevertheless he refused to sign.

The claim adjuster had recourse to a ruse. "I am an autograph collector," he said slyly. "Unfortunately, I have not my album with me, but if you will be so kind as to sign this piece of paper which I happened to have in my pocket, you will make me very happy. When I return home, I will immediately transfer your autograph to a distinguished place in my collection."

Befuddled by the pain in his injured eye, Lem signed in order to be rid of the importunate fellow, then bent again to the task of finding his store teeth. He finally discovered them deep in the mud of the bridle path. After carefully prying the set loose, he went to a public drinking fountain for the dual purpose of bathing both it and his hurt eye.

12

While he busied himself at the fountain, a young man approached. This stranger was distinguished from the usual run by his long black hair which tumbled in waves over the back of his collar and by an unusually high and broad forehead. On his head he wore a soft, black hat with an enormously wide brim. Both his tie, which was Windsor, and his gestures, which were Latin, floated with the same graceful freedom as his hair.

"Excuse me," said this odd-appearing individual, "but I witnessed your heroic act and I wish to take the liberty of congratulating you. In these effete times, it is rare indeed for one to witness a hero in action."

Lem was embarrassed. He hurriedly replaced his teeth and thanked the stranger for his praise. He continued, however, to bathe his wounded eye, which was still giving him considerable pain.

"Let me introduce myself," the young man continued. "I am Sylvanus Snodgrasse, a poet both by vocation and avocation. May I ask your name?"

"Lemuel Pitkin," answered our hero, making no attempt to hide the fact that he was suspicious of this self-styled "poet." In fact there were many things about him that reminded Lem of Mr. Wellington Mape.

"Mr. Pitkin," he said grandly, "I intend to write an ode about the deed performed by you this day. You do not perhaps appreciate, having a true hero's modesty, the significance, the classicality—if I may be permitted a neologism—of your performance. Poor Boy, Flying Team, Banker's Daughter . . . it's in the real American tradition and perfectly fitted to my native lyre. Fie on your sickly Prousts, U.S. poets must write about the U.S."

Our hero did not venture to comment on these sentiments. For one thing, his eye hurt so much that even his sense of hearing was occupied with the pain.

Snodgrasse kept talking, and soon a crowd of curious people gathered around him and poor Lemuel. The "poet" no longer addressed our hero, but the crowd in general.

"Gentlemen," said he in a voice that carried all the way to Central Park South, "and ladies, I am moved by this youth's heroism to venture a few remarks.

"There have been heroes before him—Leonidas, Quintus Maximus, Wolfe Tone, Deaf Smith, to mention only a few —but this should not prevent us from hailing L. Pitkin as the hero, if not of our time, at least of the immediate past.

"One of the most striking things about his heroism is the dominance of the horse motif, involving, as it does, not one but two horses. This is important because the depression has made all us Americans conscious of certain spiritual lacks, not the least of which is the symbolic horse.

"Every great nation has its symbolic horses. The grandeur that was Greece is made immortal by those marvelous equines, half god, half beast, still to be seen in the corners of the Parthenon pediment. Rome, the eternal city, how perfectly is her glory caught in those martial steeds that rear their fearful forms to Titus's triumph! And Venice, Queen of the Adriatic, has she not her winged sea horses, kindred to both air and water?

"Alas, only we are without. Do not point to General

Sherman's horse or I will be angry, for that craven hack, that crowbait, is nothing. I repeat, nothing. What I want is for all my hearers to go home and immediately write to their congressmen demanding that a statue depicting Pitkin's heroic act be erected in every public park throughout our great country."

Although Sylvanus Snodgrasse kept on in this vein for quite some time, I will stop reporting his oration to acquaint you, dear reader, with his real purpose. As you have probably surmised, it was not so innocent as it seemed. The truth is that while he kept the crowd amused, his confederates circulated freely among its members and picked their pockets.

They had succeeded in robbing the whole crowd, including our hero, when a policeman made his appearance. Snodgrasse immediately discontinued his address and hurried off after his henchmen.

The officer dispersed the gathering and everyone moved away except Lem, who was lying on the ground in a dead faint. The bluecoat, thinking that the poor boy was drunk, kicked him a few times, but when several hard blows in the groin failed to budge him, he decided to call an ambulance.

13

One wintry morning, several weeks after the incident in the park, Lem was dismissed from the hospital minus his right eye. It had been so severely damaged that the physicians had thought best to remove it.

He had no money, for, as we have recounted, Snod grasse's henchmen had robbed him. Even the teeth that Warden Purdy had given him were gone. They had been taken from him by the hospital authorities, who claimed that they did not fit properly and were therefore a menace to his health.

The poor lad was standing on a windy corner, not knowing which way to turn, when he saw a man in a coonskin hat. This remarkable headgear made Lem stare, and the more he looked the more the man seemed to resemble Shagpoke Whipple.

It was Mr. Whipple. Lem hastened to call out to him, and the ex-President stopped to shake hands with his young friend.

"About those inventions," Shagpoke said immediately after they had finished greeting each other. "It was too bad that you left the penitentiary before I could hand them over to you. Not knowing your whereabouts, I perfected them myself.

"But let us repair to a coffee place," he added, changing the subject, "where we can talk over your prospects together. I am still very much interested in your career. In fact, my young friend, America has never had a greater need for her youth than in these parlous times."

After our hero had thanked him for his interest and good wishes, Mr. Whipple continued to talk. "Speaking of coffee," he said, "did you know that the fate of our country was decided in the coffee shops of Boston during the hectic days preceding the late rebellion?"

As they paused at the door of a restaurant, Mr. Whipple asked Lem still another question. "By the way," he said, "I am temporarily without funds. Are you able to meet the obligation we will incur in this place?"

"No," replied Lem, sadly, "I am penniless."

"That's different," said Mr. Whipple with a profound sigh. "In that case we will go where I have credit."

Lem was conducted by his fellow townsman to an extremely poor section of the city. After standing on line for several hours, they each received a doughnut and a cup of coffee from the Salvation Army lassie in charge. They then sat down on the curb to eat their little snack.

"You are perhaps wondering," Shagpoke began, "how it is that I stand on line with these homeless vagrants to obtain bad coffee and soggy doughnuts. Be assured that I do it of my own free will and for the good of the state."

Here he paused long enough to skillfully "shoot a snipe" that was still burning. He puffed contentedly on his catch.

"When I left jail, it was my intention to run for office again. But I discovered to my great amazement and utter horror that my party, the Democratic Party, carried not a single plank in its platform that I could honestly endorse. Rank socialism was and is rampant. How could I, Shagpoke Whipple, ever bring myself to accept a program which promised to take from American citizens their inalienable birthright; the right to sell their labor and their children's labor without restrictions as to either price or hours?

"The time for a new party with the old American principles was, I realized, overripe. I decided to form it; and so the National Revolutionary Party, popularly known as the 'Leather Shirts,' was born. The uniform of our 'Storm Troops' is a coonskin cap like the one I am wearing, a deerskin shirt and a pair of moccasins. Our weapon is the squirrel rifle."

He pointed to the long queue of unemployed who stood waiting before the Salvation Army canteen. "These men," he said, "are the material from which I must fill the ranks of my party."

With all the formality of a priest, Shagpoke turned to our hero and laid his hand on his shoulder.

"My boy," he said, and his voice broke under the load of emotion it was forced to bear, "my boy, will you join me?"

"Certainly, sir," said Lem, a little unsurely.

"Excellent!" exclaimed Mr. Whipple. "Excellent! I here-
with appoint you a commander attached to my general
staff."

He drew himself up and saluted Lem, who was startled
by the gesture.

"Commander Pitkin," he ordered briskly, "I desire to address these people. Please obtain a soapbox."

Our hero went on the errand required of him, and soon
returned with a large box, which Mr. Whipple immediately
mounted. He then set about attracting the attention of the
vagrants collected about the Salvation Army canteen by
shouting:

"Remember the River Raisin!

"Remember the Alamo!

"Remember the Maine!"
and many other famous slogans.

When a large group had gathered, Shagpoke began his
harangue.

"I'm a simple man," he said with great simplicity, "and I
want to talk to you about simple things. You'll get no high-
falutin talk from me.

"First of all, you people want jobs. Isn't that so?"

An ominous rumble of assent came from the throats of
the poorly dressed gathering.

"Well, that's the only and prime purpose of the National
Revolutionary Party—to get jobs for everyone. There was
enough work to go around in 1927, why isn't there enough
now? I'll tell you; because of the Jewish international
bankers and the Bolshevik labor unions, that's why. It was
those two agents that did the most to hinder American
business and to destroy its glorious expansion. The former
because of their hatred of America and love for Europe
and the latter because of their greed for higher and still
higher wages.

"What is the role of the labor union today? It is a privileged club which controls all the best jobs for its members. When one of you applies for a job, even if the man who owns the plant wants to hire you, do you get it? Not if you haven't got a union card. Can any tyranny be greater? Has Liberty ever been more brazenly despised?"

These statements were received with cheers by his audience.

"Citizens, Americans," Mr. Whipple continued, when the noise had subsided, "we of the middle class are being crushed between two gigantic millstones. Capital is the upper stone and Labor the lower, and between them we suffer and die, ground out of existence.

"Capital is international; its home is in London and in Amsterdam. Labor is international; its home is in Moscow. We alone are American; and when we die, America dies.

"When I say that, I make no idle boast, for history bears me out. Who but the middle class left aristocratic Europe to settle on these shores? Who but the middle class, the small farmers and storekeepers, the clerks and petty officials, fought for freedom and died that America might escape from British tyranny?

"This is our country and we must fight to keep it so. If America is ever again to be great, it can only be through the triumph of the revolutionary middle class.

"We must drive the Jewish international bankers out of Wall Street! We must destroy the Bolshevik labor unions! We must purge our country of all the alien elements and ideas that now infest her!

"America for Americans! Back to the principles of Andy Jackson and Abe Lincoln!"

Here Shagpoke paused to let the cheers die down, then called for volunteers to join his "Storm Battalions."

A number of men came forward. In their lead was a very dark individual, who had extra-long black hair of an extremely coarse quality, and on whose head was a derby hat many sizes too small for him.

"Me American mans," he announced proudly. "Me got heap coon hat, two maybe six. By, by catchum plenty more coon maybe." With this he grinned from ear to ear.

But Shagpoke was a little suspicious of his complexion, and looked at him with disfavor. In the South, where he expected to get considerable support for his movement, they would not stand for Negroes.

The good-natured stranger seemed to sense what was wrong, for he said, "Me Injun, mister, me chief along my people. Gotum gold mine, oil well. Name of Jake Raven. Ugh!"

Shagpoke grew cordial at once. "Chief Jake Raven," he said, holding out his hand, "I am happy to welcome you into our organization. We 'Leather Shirts' can learn much from your people, fortitude, courage and relentless purpose among other things."

After taking down his name, Shagpoke gave the Indian a card which read as follows:

EZRA SILVERBLATT
Official Tailor
to the
NATIONAL REVOLUTIONARY PARTY
Coonskin hats with extra long tails, deerskin shirts with or without fringes, blue jeans, moccasins, squirrel rifles, everything for the American Fascist at rock bottom prices. 30% off for Cash.

But let us leave Mr. Whipple and Lem busy with their recruiting to observe the actions of a certain member of the crowd.

The individual in question would have been remarkable in any gathering, and among the starved, ragged men that surrounded Shagpoke, he stuck out like the proverbial sore thumb. For one thing he was fat, enormously fat. There were other fat men present to be sure, but they were yellow, unhealthy, while this man's fat was pink and shone with health.

On his head was a magnificent bowler hat. It was a beautiful jet in color, and must have cost more than twelve dollars. He was snugly encased in a tight-fitting Chesterfield overcoat with a black velvet collar. His stiff-bosomed shirt had light gray bars, and his tie was of some rich but sober material in black and white pin-checks. Spats, rattan stick and yellow gloves completed his outfit.

This elaborate fat man tiptoed out of the crowd and made his way to a telephone booth in a nearby drug store, where he called two numbers.

His conversation with the person answering his first call, a Wall Street exchange, went something like this:

"Operative 6384XM, working out of the Bourse, Paris, France. Middle-class organizers functioning on unemployed front, corner of Houston and Bleecker Streets."

"Thank you, 6384XM, what is your estimate?"

"Twenty men and a fire hose."

"At once, 6384XM, at once."

His second call was to an office near Union Square.

"Comrade R, please. . . . Comrade R?"

"Yes."

"Comrade R, this is Comrade Z speaking. Gay Pay Oo, Moscow, Russia. Middle-class organizers recruiting on the corner of Houston and Bleecker Streets."

"Your estimate, comrade, for liquidation of said activities?"

"Ten men with lead pipes and brass knuckles to cooperate with Wall Street office of the I.J.B."

"No bombs required?"

"No, comrade."

"Der Tag!"

"Der Tag!"

Mr. Whipple had just enrolled his twenty-seventh recruit, when the forces of both the international Jewish
bankers and the Communists converged on his meeting.
They arrived in high-powered black limousines and de-
ployed through the streets with a skill which showed long
and careful training in that type of work. In fact their
officers were all West Point graduates.

Mr. Whipple saw them coming, but like a good general
his first thoughts were for his men.

"The National Revolutionary Party will now go under-
ground!" he shouted.

Lem, made wary by his past experiences with the police,
immediately took to his heels, followed by Chief Raven.
Shagpoke, however, was late in getting started. He still
had one foot on the soapbox when he was hit a terrific
blow on the head with a piece of lead pipe.

14

"My man, if you can wear this glass eye, I have a job for
you."

The speaker was an exceedingly dapper gentleman in a
light gray fedora hat and a pince-nez with a black silk rib-
bon that fell to his coat opening in a graceful loop.

As he spoke, he held out at arm's length a beautiful glass
eye.

But the object of his words did not reply; it did not
even move. To anyone but a trained observer, he would
have appeared to be addressing a bundle of old rags that
someone had propped up on a park bench.

Turning the eye from side to side, so that it sparkled like

a jewel in the winter sun, the man waited patiently for the bundle to reply. From time to time, he stirred it sharply with the Malacca walking stick he carried.

Suddenly a groan came from the rags and they shook sightly. The cane had evidently reached a sensitive spot. Encouraged, the man repeated his original proposition.

"Can you wear this eye? If so, I'll hire you."

At this, the bundle gave a few spasmodic quivers and a faint whimper. From somewhere below its peak a face appeared, then a greenish hand moved out and took the glittering eye, raising it to an empy socket in the upper part of the face.

"Here, let me help you," said the owner of the eye kindly. With a few deft motions he soon had it fixed in its proper receptacle.

"Perfect!" exclaimed the man, standing back and admiring his handiwork. "Perfect! You're hired!"

He then reached into his overcoat and brought forth a wallet from which he extracted a five-dollar bill and a calling card. He laid both of these on the bench beside the one-eyed man, who by now had again become a quiescent bundle of greasy rags.

"Get yourself a haircut, a bath and a big meal, then go to my tailors, Ephraim Pierce and Sons, and they will fit you out with clothes. When you are presentable, call on me at the Ritz Hotel."

With these words, the man in the gray fedora turned sharply on his heel and left the park.

If you have not already guessed the truth, dear reader, let me acquaint you with the fact that the bundle of rags contained our hero, Lemuel Pitkin. Alas, to such a sorry pass had he come.

After the unfortunate termination of Shagpoke's attempt to recruit men for his "Leather Shirts," he had rapidly gone from bad to worse. Having no money and no way in which to obtain any, he had wandered from employment agency to employment agency without success. Reduced to eating from garbage pails and sleeping in empty lots, he had become progressively shabbier and weaker, until he had reached the condition we discovered him in at the beginning of this chapter.

But now things were looking up again, and just in time I must admit, for our hero had begun to doubt whether he would ever make his fortune.

Lem pocketed the five dollars that the stranger had left and examined the card.

ELMER HAINEY, ESQUIRE
RITZ HOTEL

This was all the bit of engraved pasteboard said. It gave no evidence of either the gentleman's business or profession. But this did not in any way bother Lem, for at last it looked as though he were going to have a job; and in the year of our Lord nineteen thirty-four that was indeed something.

Lem struggled to his feet and set out to follow Mr. Hainey's instructions. In fact he ate two large meals and took two baths. It was only his New England training that prevented him from getting two haircuts.

Having done as much as he could to rehabilitate his body, he next went to the shop of Ephraim Pierce and Sons, where he was fitted out with a splendid wardrobe complete in every detail. Several hours later, he walked up Park Avenue to wait on his new employer, looking every inch a prosperous young businessman of the finest type.

When Lem asked for Mr. Hainey, the manager of the Ritz bowed him into the elevator, which stopped to let him off at the fortieth floor. He rang the doorbell of Mr. Hainey's suite and in a few minutes was ushered into that gentleman's presence by an English personal servant.

Mr. Hainey greeted the lad with great cordiality. "Excellent! Excellent!" he repeated three or four times in rapid succession as he inspected the transformed appearance of our hero.

Lem expressed his gratitude by a deep bow.

"If there is anything about your outfit that you dislike," he went on to say, "please tell me now before I give you your instructions."

Emboldened by his kind manner, Lem ventured an objection. "Pardon me, sir," he said, "but the eye, the glass eye you gave me is the wrong color. My good eye is blue-gray, while the one you provided me with is light green."

"Exactly," was Mr. Hainey's surprising answer. "The effect is, as I calculated, striking. When anyone sees you I want to make sure that they notice that one of your eyes is glass."

Lem was forced to agree to this strange idea and he did so with all the grace he could manage.

Mr. Hainey then got down to business. His whole manner changed, becoming as cold as a steel trap and twice as formal.

"My secretary," he said, "has typed a set of instructions which I will give you tonight. I want you to take them home and study them carefully, for you will be expected to do exactly as they order without the slightest deviation. One slip, please remember, and you will be immediately discharged."

"Thank you, sir," replied Lem. "I understand."

"Your salary," said Mr. Hainey, softening a bit, "will be thirty dollars a week and found. I have arranged room and board for you at the Warford House. Please go there tonight."

Mr. Hainey then took out his wallet and gave Lem three ten-dollar bills.

"You are very generous," said Lem, taking them. "I shall do my utmost to satisfy you."

"That's nice, but please don't show too much zeal, simply follow instructions."

Mr. Hainey next went to his desk and took from it several typewritten sheets of paper. He gave these to Lem.

"One more thing," he said, shaking hands at the door, "you may be a little mystified when you read your instructions, but that cannot be helped, for I am unable to give you a complete explanation at this time. However, I want you to know that I own a glass eye factory, and that your duties are part of a sales-promotion campaign."

15

Lem restrained his curiosity. He waited until he was safely ensconced in his new quarters in the Warford House before opening the instructions Mr. Hainey had given him.

Here is what he read:

"Go to the jewelry store of Hazelton Frères and ask to see their diamond stickpins. After looking at one tray, demand to see another. While the clerk has his back turned, remove the glass eye from your head and put it in your pocket. As soon as the clerk turns around again, appear to be searching frantically on the floor for something.

"The following dialogue will then take place:

"*Clerk:* 'Have you lost something, sir?'

"*You:* 'Yes, my eye.' (Here indicate the opening in your head with your index finger.)

"*Clerk:* 'That's unfortunate, sir. I'll help you look, sir.'

"*You:* 'Please do. (With much agitation.) I must find it.'

"A thorough search of the premises is then made, but of course the missing eye cannot be found because it is safe in your pocket.

"*You:* 'Please may I see one of the owners of this store; one of the Hazelton Brothers?' (Note: Frères means brothers and is not to be mistaken for the storekeeper's last name.)

"In a few minutes the clerk will bring Mr. Hazelton from his office in the rear of the store.

"*You:* 'Mr. Hazelton, sir, I have had the misfortune to lose my eye here in your shop.'

"*Mr. Hazelton:* 'Perhaps you left it at home.'

"*You:* 'Impossible! I would have felt the draft for I walked here from Mr. Hamilton Schuyler's house on Fifth Avenue. No, I'm afraid that it was in its proper position when I entered your place.'

"*Mr. Hazelton:* 'You can be certain, sir, that we will make a thorough search.'

"*You:* 'Please do. I am, however, unable to wait the outcome of your efforts. I have to be in the Spanish embassy to see the ambassador, Count Raymon de Guzman y Alfrache (the y is pronounced like the e in eat) within the hour.'

"Mr. Hazelton will bow profoundly on hearing with whom your appointment is.

"*You* (continuing): 'The eye I have lost is irreplaceable. It was made for me by a certain German expert, and cost a very large sum. I cannot get another because its maker was killed in the late war and the secret of its manufacture was buried with him. (Pause for a brief moment, bowing your head as though in sorrow for the departed expert.) However (you continue), please tell your clerks that I will pay one thousand dollars as a reward to anyone who recovers my eye.'

"*Mr. Hazelton:* 'That will be entirely unnecessary, sir. Rest assured that we will do everything in our power to discover it for you.'

"*You:* 'Very good. I am going to visit friends on Long

Island tonight, but I will be in your shop tomorrow. If you have the eye, I will insist on paying the reward.'

"Mr. Hazelton will then bow you out of the shop.

"Until you receive further instructions from Mr. Hainey, you are to stay away from the near vicinity of Hazelton Frères.

"On the day following your visit to the shop call the Ritz Hotel and ask for Mr. Hainey's secretary. Tell him whether or not everything went off in accordance with these instructions. The slightest deviation on the part of Mr. Hazelton from the prescribed formula must be reported."

16

Lem's job was a sinecure. He had merely to enact the same scene over one morning a week, each time in a different store. He soon had his part by heart, and once he had lost his embarrassment over having to say that he knew the Spanish Ambassador, he quite enjoyed his work. It reminded him of the amateur theatricals he had participated in at the Ottsville High School.

Then, too, his position permitted him a great deal of leisure. He used this spare time to good advantage by visiting the many interesting spots for which New York City is justly famous.

He also made an unsuccessful attempt to find Mr. Whipple. At the Salvation Army post they told him that they had observed Mr. Whipple lying quietly in the gutter after the meeting of the "Leather Shirts," but that when they looked the next day to see if he were still there they found only a large blood stain. Lem looked himself but failed even to find this stain, there being many cats in the neighborhood.

He was a sociable youth and quickly made friends with several of the other guests of the Warford House. None of them were his age, however, so that he was pleased when a young man named Samuel Perkins spoke to him.

Sam worked in a furnishing goods store on lower Broadway. He was very fond of dress and indulged in a variety of showy neckties, being able to get them at reduced rates.

"What line are you in?" he asked our hero in the lobby one evening while they were waiting for the supper bell to ring.

"I'm in the glass business," Lem answered cautiously, for he had been warned not to explain his duties to anyone.

"How much do you get?" was the forward youth's next question.

"Thirty dollars a week and found," said Lem, honestly.

"I get thirty-five without keep, but it's too little for me. A man can't live on that kind of money, what with the opera once a week and decent clothes. Why, my carfare alone comes to over a dollar, not counting taxicabs."

"Yes, it must be rather a tight squeeze for you," said Lem with a smile as he thought of all the large families who lived on smaller incomes than Mr. Perkins'.

"Of course," Sam went on, "the folks at home allow me another ten dollars a week. You see the old gent has money. But I tell you it sure melts away in this town."

"No doubt," said Lem. "There are a good many ways to spend money here."

"Suppose we go to the theater tonight?"

"No," Lem replied, "I'm not as fortunate as you are. I have no wealthy father to fall back on and must save the little I earn."

"Well, then," said Sam, for that youth could not live without excitement of some sort, "what do you say we visit Chinatown? It'll only cost us carfare."

To this proposition Lem readily agreed. "I'd like very much to go," he said. "Perhaps Mr. Warren would like to join us."

Mr. Warren was another guest whose acquaintance Lem had made.

"What, that crank!" exclaimed Sam, who was by way of being somewhat of a snob. "He's soft in his upper story. Pretends that he's literary and writes for the magazines."

"He does, doesn't he?"

"Very likely, but did you ever see such shabby neckties as he wears?"

"He hasn't your advantages for getting them," said Lem with a smile, for he knew where the young man worked.

"How do you like the tie I have on? It's a stunner, isn't it?" asked Sam complacently.

"It's very striking," said Lem, whose tastes were much more sober.

"I get a new necktie every week. You see, I get them at half price. The girls always notice a fellow's necktie."

The supper bell sounded, and the two youths parted to go to their own tables. After eating, they met again in the lobby and proceeded to Chinatown.

17

Lem and his new friend wandered through Mott Street and its environs, observing with considerable interest the curious customs and outlandish manners of that neighborhood's large oriental population.

Early in the evening, however, an incident occurred which made our hero feel sorry that he had ventured out with Sam Perkins. When they came upon an ancient celestial, who was quietly reading a newspaper under an arc lamp, Sam accosted him before Lem could interfere.

"Hey, John," said the youth mockingly, "no tickee, no washee." And he laughed foolishly in the manner of his kind.

The almond-eyed old man looked up from his newspaper

and stared coldly at him for a full minute, then said with great dignity, "By the blessed beard of my grandfather, you're the lousiest pimple-faced ape I ever did see."

At this Sam made as though to strike the aged oriental. But that surprising individual was not in the least frightened. He took a small hatchet out of his pocket and proceeded to shave the hair from the back of his hand with its razor-sharp edge.

Sam turned quite pale and began to bluster until Lem thought it best to intervene.

But even his lesson in manners had no effect on the brash youth. He so persisted in his unmannerly conduct that our hero was tempted to part company with him.

Sam stopped in front of what was evidently an unlicensed liquor parlor.

"Come on in," he said, "and have a whisky."

"Thank you," said our hero, "but I don't care for whisky."

"Perhaps you prefer beer?"

"I don't care to drink anything, thank you."

"You don't mean to say you're a temperance crank?"

"Yes, I think I am."

"Oh, go to the devil, you prude," said Sam, ringing a signal button that was secreted in the door of the "blind pig."

To Lem's great relief, he at last found himself alone. It was still early, so he decided to continue his stroll.

He turned a corner not far from Pell Street, when, suddenly, a bottle smashed at his feet, missing his skull by inches.

Was it intentional or accidental?

Lem looked around carefully. The street was deserted and all the houses that faced on it had their blinds drawn. He noticed that the only store front on the block carried a sign reading, "Wu Fong, Wet Wash Laundry," but that meant nothing to him.

When he looked closer at the bottle, he was surprised to see a sheet of notepaper between the bits of shattered glass and stooped to pick it up.

At this the door of the laundry opened noiselessly to emit one of Wu Fong's followers, an enormous Chinaman. His felt slippers were silent on the pavement, and as he crept up on our hero, something glittered in his hand.

It was a knife.

18

Many chapters earlier in this book, we left our heroine, Betty Prail, in the bad house of Wu Fong, awaiting the visit of a pockmarked Armenian from Malta.

Since then numbers of orientals, Slavs, Latins, Celts and Semites had visited her, sometimes as many as three in one night. However, so large a number was rare because Wu Fong held her at a price much above that of the other female inmates.

Naturally enough, Betty was not quite as happy in her situation as was Wu Fong. At first she struggled against the series of "husbands" that were forced on her, but when all her efforts proved futile she adapted herself as best she could to her onerous duties. Nevertheless, she was continuously seeking a method of escape.

It was Betty, of course, who had authored the note in the bottle. She had been standing at her window, thinking with horror of the impending visit of a heavyweight wrestler called Selim Hammid Bey, who claimed to be in love with her, when she suddenly saw Lem Pitkin turn the corner and pass in front of the laundry. She had hastily written a note describing her predicament, and putting it into a bottle had tossed it into the street.

But, unfortunately, her action had not gone unobserved. One of Wu Fong's many servants had been carefully watching her through the keyhole, and had immediately carried the intelligence to his master, who had sent the enormous Chinaman after Lem with a knife.

Before I take up where I left off in my last chapter, there are several changes in Wu Fong's establishment which I would like to report. These changes seem significant to me, and while their bearing on this story may not be obvious, still I believe it does exist.

The depression hit Wu Fong as hard as it did more respectable merchants, and like them he decided that he was over-stocked. In order to cut down, he would have to specialize and could no longer run a "House of All Nations."

Wu Fong was a very shrewd man and a student of fashions. He saw that the trend was in the direction of home industry and home talent, and when the Hearst papers began their "Buy American" campaign he decided to get rid of all the foreigners in his employ and turn his establishment into an hundred per centum American place.

Although in 1928 it would have been exceedingly difficult for him to have obtained the necessary girls, by 1934 things were different. Many respectable families of genuine native stock had been reduced to extreme poverty and had thrown their female children on the open market.

He engaged Mr. Asa Goldstein to redecorate the house and that worthy designed a Pennsylvania Dutch, Old South, Log Cabin Pioneer, Victorian New York, Western Cattle Days, California Monterey, Indian, and Modern Girl series of interiors. In general the results were as follows:

Lena Haubengrauber from Perkiomen Creek, Bucks County, Pennsylvania. Her rooms were filled with painted pine furniture and decorated with slip ware, spatter ware, chalk ware and "Gaudy Dutch." Her simple farm dress was fashioned of bright gingham.

Alice Sweethorne from Paducah, Kentucky. Besides many fine pieces of old Sheraton from Savannah, in her suite there was a wonderful iron grille from Charleston whose beauty of workmanship made every visitor gasp with pleasure. She wore a ball gown of the Civil War period.

Mary Judkins from Jugtown Hill, Arkansas. Her walls were lined with oak puncheons chinked with mud. Her mattress was stuffed with field corn and covered by a buffalo rope. There was real dirt on her floors. She was dressed in homespun, butternut stained, and wore a pair of men's boots.

Patricia Van Riis from Gramercy Park, Manhattan, New York City. Her suite was done in the style known as Biedermeier. The windows were draped with thirty yards of white velvet apiece and the chandelier in her sitting room had over eight hundred crystal pendants attached to it. She was dressed like an early "Gibson Girl."

Powder River Rose from Carson's Store, Wyoming. Her apartment was the replica of a ranch bunkhouse. Strewn around it in well-calculated confusion were such miscellaneous articles as spurs, saddle blankets, straw, guitars, quirts, pearl-handled revolvers, hayforks and playing cards. She wore goatskin chaps, a silk blouse and a five-gallon hat with a rattlesnake band.

Dolores O'Riely from Alta Vista, California. In order to save money, Wu Fong had moved her into the suite that had been occupied by Conchita, the Spanish girl. He merely substituted a Mission chair for the horsehide one with the steer-horn arms and called it "Monterey." Asa Goldstein was very angry when he found out, but Wu Fong refused to do anything more about it, because he felt that she was bound to be a losing proposition. The style, he said was not obviously enough American even in its most authentic forms.

Princess Roan Fawn from Two Forks, Oklahoma Indian Reservation, Oklahoma. Her walls were papered with birch bark to make it look like a wigwam and she did business on the floor. Except for a necklace of wolf's teeth, she was naked under her bull's-eye blanket.

Miss Cobina Wiggs from Woodstock, Connecticut. She lived in one large room that was a combination of a locker in an athletic club and the office of a mechanical draughtsman. Strewn around were parts of an aeroplane, T-squares, callipers, golf clubs, books, gin bottles, hunting horns and paintings by modern masters. She had broad shoulders, no hips and very long legs. Her costume was an aviator's jumper complete with helmet attached. It was made of silver cloth and fitted very tightly.

Betty Prail from Ottsville, Vermont. Her furnishings and costume have already been described, and it should suffice to say here that they remained untouched.

These were not the only vital changes Wu Fong made in his establishment. He was as painstaking as a great artist, and in order to be as consistent as one he did away with the French cuisine and wines traditional to his business. Instead, he substituted an American kitchen and cellar.

When a client visited Lena Haubengrauber, it was possible for him to eat roast groundhog and drink Sam Thompson rye. While with Alice Sweethorne, he was served sow belly with grits and bourbon. In Mary Judkins' rooms he received, if he so desired, fried squirrel and corn liquor. In the suite occupied by Patricia Van Riis, lobster and champagne wine were the rule. The patrons of Powder River Rose usually ordered mountain oysters and washed them down with forty-rod. And so on down the list: while with Dolores O'Riely, tortillas and prune brandy from the Imperial Valley; while with Princess Roan Fawn, baked dog and firewater; while with Betty Prail, fish chowder and Jamaica rum. Finally, those who sought the favors of the "Modern Girl," Miss Cobina Wiggs, were regaled with tomato and lettuce sandwiches and gin.

19

The enormous Chinaman with the uplifted knife did not bring it down, because he had been struck by a sudden thought. While he debated the pros and cons of his idea over in his mind, the unsuspecting youth picked up the note Betty had thrown at him.

> "*Dear Mr. Pitkin—*" he read.
> "*I am held captive. Please save me.*
> *Your grateful friend,*
> *Elizabeth Prail.*"

When our hero had thoroughly digested the contents of the little missive, he turned to look for a policeman. It was this that made the Chinaman decide on a course of action. He dropped the knife, and with a skillful oriental trick that took our hero entirely by surprise pinned Lem's arms in such a way as to render him helpless.

He then whistled through his nose in coolie fashion. In obedience to this signal several more of Wu Fong's followers came running to his assistance. Although Lem struggled valiantly, he was overpowered and forced to enter the laundry.

Lem's captors dragged him into the presence of the sinister Wu Fong, who rubbed his hands gleefully as he inspected the poor lad.

"You have done well, Chin Lao Tse," he said, praising the man who had captured Lem.

"I demand to be set free!" expostulated our hero. "You have no right to keep me here."

But the crafty oriental ignored his protests and smiled inscrutably. He could well use a nice-looking American boy. That very night, he expected a visit from the Maharajah of Kanurani, whose tastes were notorious. Wu Fong congratulated himself; the gods were indeed good.

"Prepare him," said he in Chinese.

The poor lad was taken to a room that had been fitted out like a ship's cabin. The walls were paneled in teak, and there were sextants, compasses and other such gear in profusion. His captors then forced him to don a tight-fitting sailor suit. After warning him in no uncertain terms not to try to escape, they left him to his own devices.

Lem sat on the edge of a bunk that was built into one corner of the room with his head buried in his hands. He wondered what new ordeal fate had in store for him, but being unable to guess he thought of other things.

Would he lose his job if he failed to report to Mr. Hainey? Probably, yes. Where was his dear mother? Probably in the poorhouse, or begging from door to door, if she were not dead. Where was Mr. Whipple? Dead and buried in Potter's Field more than likely. And how could he get a message to Miss Prail?

Lem was still trying to solve this last problem when Chin Lao Tse, the man who had captured him, entered the room, carrying a savage-looking automatic in his hand.

"Listen, boy," he said menacingly, "see this gat? Well, if you don't behave I'll drill you clean."

Chin then proceeded to secrete himself in a closet. Before closing the door, he showed Lem that he intended to watch his every move through the keyhole.

The poor lad racked his brains, but could not imagine what was wanted of him. He was soon to find out, however.

There was a knock on the door and Wu Fong entered

followed by a little dark man whose hands were covered with jewels. It was the Maharajah of Kanurani.

"My, wath a pithy thailer boy," lisped the Indian prince with unfeigned delight.

"I'm extremely happy that he finds favor in your august eyes, excellency," said Wu Fong with a servile bow, after which he backed out of the room.

The Maharajah minced up to our hero, who was conscious only of the man in the closet, and put his arm around the lad's waist.

"Thom on, pithy boy, giff me a kith," he said with a leer that transfigured his otherwise unremarkable visage into a thing of evil.

A wave of disgust made Lem's hair stand on end. "Does he think me a girl?" the poor lad wondered. "No, he called me a boy at least twice."

Lem looked towards the closet for instructions. The man in that receptacle opened his door and poked his head out. Puckering up his lips, he rolled his eyes amorously, at the same time pointing at the Indian Prince.

When our hero realized what was expected of him, he turned pale with horror. He looked again at the Maharajah and what he saw of lust in that man's eyes made him almost swoon.

Fortunately for Lem, however, instead of swooning, he opened his mouth to scream. This was the only thing that could have saved him, for he spread his jaws too wide and his store teeth fell clattering to the carpet.

The Maharajah jumped away in disgust.

Then another lucky accident occurred. When Lem bent awkwardly to pick up his teeth, the glass eye that Mr. Hainey had given him popped from his head and smashed to smithereens on the floor.

This last was too much for the Maharajah of Kanurani.

He became enraged. Wu Fong had cheated him! What kind of a pretty boy was this that came apart so horribly?

Livid with anger, the Indian prince ran out of the room to demand his money back. After he had gotten it, he left the house, vowing never to return.

Wu Fong blamed the loss of the Maharajah's trade on Lem and was extremely vexed with the poor lad. He ordered his men to beat him roundly, strip him of his sailor suit, then throw him into the street with his clothes after him.

20

Lem gathered together his clothing and crawled into the areaway of a deserted house, where he donned his things. His first thought was to find a policeman.

As is usual in such circumstances, a guardian of the law was not immediately forthcoming and he had to go several miles before he found a "peeler."

"Officer," said our hero as best he could minus his oral equipment, "I want to lodge a complaint."

"Yes," said Patrolman Riley shortly, for the poor lad's appearance was far from prepossessing. The Chinaman had torn his clothing and his eye was gone as well as his teeth.

"I want you to summon reinforcements, then immediately arrest Wu Fong who is running a disorderly house under the guise of a laundry."

"Wu Fong is it that you want me to arrest? Why, you drunken fool, he's the biggest man in the district. Take my advice and get yourself a cup of black coffee, then go home and sleep it off."

"But I have positive proof that he's keeping a girl in his house against her will, and he did me physical violence."

"One more word out of you about my great good friend," said the officer, "and off you go to jail."

"But . . ." began Lem indignantly.

Officer Riley was a man of his word. He did not let the poor lad finish, but struck him a smart blow on the head with his truncheon, then took him by the collar and dragged him to the station house.

When Lem regained consciousness several hours later, he found himself in a cell. He quickly remembered what had happened to him and tried to think of a way in which to extricate himself from his difficulties. The first thing was to tell his story to some superior police officer or magistrate. But no matter how loudly he called, he was unable to attract the attention of anyone.

Not until the next day was he fed, and then a small man of the Jewish persuasion entered his cell.

"Have you any money?" said this member of the chosen people.

"Who are you?" countered Lem with another question.

"Me? I'm your lawyer, Seth Abromovitz, Esquire. Please answer my first question or I won't be able to handle your case properly."

"My case?" queried Lem in astonishment. "I've done nothing."

"Ignorance of the law is no defense," said Lawyer Abromovitz pompously.

"Of what am I accused?" asked the poor lad in confusion.

"Of several things. Disorderly conduct and assaulting a police officer, for one; of conspiring to overthrow the Government, for two; and last but not least, of using the glim racket to mulct storekeepers."

"But I didn't do any of these things," protested Lem.

"Listen, bud," said the lawyer, dropping all formality. "I'm not the judge, you don't have to lie to me. You're One-eyed Pitkin, the glim dropper, and you know it."

"It's true that I have but one eye, but . . ."

"But me no buts. This is a tough case. That is, unless you can grow an eye overnight in that hole in your mug."

"I am innocent," repeated Lem sadly.

"If that's the line you intend to take, I wouldn't be surprised if you got life. But tell me, didn't you go to the store of Hazelton Frères and make believe you lost your eye?"

"Yes," said Lem, "but I didn't take anything or do anything."

"Didn't you offer a reward of one thousand dollars for the return of your eye?"

"Yes, but . . ."

"Again, but. Please don't but me no buts. Your accomplice went around the next day and made believe he had found a glass eye on the floor of the store. Mr. Hazelton said that he knew who it belonged to and asked him for the eye. He refused to give it up, saying that it looked like a very valuable eye to him and that if Mr. Hazelton would give him the address of the man who owned it, he would return the eye himself. Mr. Hazelton thought that he was going to lose all chances of collecting the thousand-dollar reward, so he offered the man a hundred dollars for the eye. After some bargaining your accomplice went out with two hundred and fifty dollars, and Mr. Hazelton is still waiting for you to come and claim your eye."

"I didn't know about all that or I wouldn't have taken the job even if I was starving," said Lem. "I was told that it was a promotion idea for a glass eye company."

"O.K., son, but I'll have to think up a little better story. Before I begin thinking, how much money have you?"

"I worked three weeks and was paid thirty dollars a week. I have ninety dollars in a savings bank."

"That's not much. This conference is going to cost you one hundred dollars with ten per cent off for cash or ninety dollars. Hand it over."

"I don't want you as my lawyer," said Lem.

"That's all right with me; but come through with the dough for this conference."

"I don't owe you anything. I didn't hire you."

"Oh, yeh, you one-eyed rat," said the lawyer, showing his true colors. "The courts appointed me and the courts will decide how much you owe me. Give me the ninety and we'll call it square. Otherwise I'll sue you."

"I'll give you nothing!" exclaimed Lem.

"Getting tough, eh? We'll soon see how tough you are. I'll tell my friend the district attorney and you'll get life."

With this last as a parting shot, Lawyer Abromovitz left our hero alone again in his cell.

21

Several days later the prosecuting attorney paid the poor lad a visit. Elisha Barnes was that official's name, and he appeared to be a rather good-natured, indolent gentleman.

"Well, son," he said, "so you're about to discover that crime doesn't pay. But, tell me, have you any money?"

"Ninety dollars," said Lem truthfully.

"That's very little, so I guess you'd better plead guilty."

"But I'm innocent," protested Lem. "Wu Fong . . ."

"Stop," interrupted Mr. Barnes, hurriedly. He had turned pale on hearing the Chinaman's name. "Take my advice and don't mention him around here."

"I'm innocent!" repeated Lem, a little desperately.

"So was Christ," said Mr. Barnes with a sigh, "and they nailed Him. However, I like you; I can see you're from New England and I'm a New Hampshire man myself. I want to help you. You've been indicted on three counts; suppose you plead guilty to one of the three and we forget the other two."

"But I'm innocent," repeated Lem again.

"Maybe, but you haven't got enough money to prove it, and besides you've got some very powerful enemies. Be sensible, plead guilty to the charge of disorderly conduct and take thirty days in the workhouse. I'll see that you don't get more. Well, what do you say?"

Our hero was silent.

"I'm giving you a fine break," Mr. Barnes went on. "If I wasn't too busy to prepare the state's case against you, I probably could get you sent away for at least fifteen years. But you see, elections are coming and I have to take part in the campaign. Besides I'm a busy man, what with this and what with that. . . . Do me a favor and maybe I can help you some time. If you make me prepare a case against you I'll get sore. I won't like you."

Lem finally agreed to do as the prosecuting attorney asked. Three days later he was sent to the workhouse for thirty days. The judge wanted to give him ninety, but Mr. Barnes lived up to his part of the bargain. He whispered something to the judge, who changed the term to the thirty days agreed upon.

A month later, when Lem was set free, he went directly to the savings bank for his ninety dollars. It was his intention to draw out the entire amount, so that he could get himself another set of false teeth and a glass eye. Without those things, he could not hope to get a job.

He presented his passbook at the paying teller's window. After a little wait, he was told that they could not give him his money because it had been attached by Seth Abromovitz. This was too much. It took all the manliness of our hero to suppress the tear that started to his good eye. With the faltering step of an old man, he stumbled out of the bank building.

Lem stood on the steps of the imposing edifice, and looked blankly at the swirling crowds that eddied past the great savings institution. Suddenly he felt a touch on his arm and a voice in his ear.

"Why so blue, duckie? How about a little fun?"

He turned mechanically and to his amazement saw that it was Betty Prail who had solicited him.

"You!" exclaimed both of the hometown friends together.

Anyone who had ever seen these two youngsters on their way home from church in Ottsville would have been struck by the great change that only a few years in the great world had made.

Miss Prail was rouged most obviously. She smelled of cheap perfume, and her dress revealed much too much of her figure. She was a woman of the streets, and an unsuccessful one at that.

As for our hero, Lemuel, minus an eye and all his teeth, he had acquired nothing but a pronounced stoop.

"How did you escape Wu Fong?" asked Lem.

"You helped me without knowing it," replied Betty. "He and his henchmen were so busy throwing you into the street that I was able to walk out of the house without anyone seeing me."

"I'm glad," said Lem.

The two young people were silent, and stood looking at each other. They both wanted to ask the same question, but they were embarrassed. Finally, they spoke at the same time.

"Have you . . ."

That was as far as they got. They both stopped to let the other finish. There was a long silence, for neither wanted to complete the question. Finally, however, they spoke again.

". . . any money?"

"No," said Lem and Betty answering the question together as they had asked it.

"I'm hungry," said Betty sadly. "I just wondered."

"I'm hungry, too," said Lem.

A policeman now approached. He had been watching them since they met.

"Get along, you rats," he said gruffly.

"I resent your talking that way to a lady," said Lem indignantly.

"What's that?" asked the officer lifting his club.

"We are both citizens of this country and you have no right to treat us in this manner," went on Lem fearlessly.

The patrolman was just about to bring his truncheon down on the lad's skull, when Betty interfered and dragged him away.

The two youngsters walked along without talking. They felt a little better together because misery loves company. Soon they found themselves in Central Park, where they sat down on a bench.

Lem sighed.

"What's the matter?" asked Betty sympathetically.

"I'm a failure," answered Lem with still another sigh.

"Why, Lemuel Pitkin, how you talk!" exclaimed Betty indignantly. "You're only seventeen going on eighteen and . . ."

"Well," interrupted Lem, a little ashamed of having admitted that he was discouraged. "I left Ottsville to make my fortune and so far I've been to jail twice and lost all my teeth and one eye."

"To make an omelette you have to break eggs," said Betty. "When you've lost both your eyes, you can talk. I read only the other day about a man who lost both of his eyes yet accumulated a fortune. I forget how, but he did. Then, too, think of Henry Ford. He was dead broke at forty and borrowed a thousand dollars from James Couzens; when he paid him back it had become thirty-eight million dollars. You're only seventeen and say you're a failure. Lem Pitkin, I'm surprised at you."

Betty continued to comfort and encourage Lem until it grew dark. With the departure of the sun, it also grew extremely cold.

From behind some shrubs that did not quite conceal him, a policeman began to eye the two young people suspiciously.

"I have nowhere to sleep," said Betty, shivering with cold.

"Nor have I," said Lem with a profound sigh.

"Let's go to the Grand Central Station," suggested Betty. "It's warm there, and I like to watch the people hurrying through. If we make believe we are waiting for a train, they won't chase us."

22

"It all seems like a dream to me, Mr. Whipple. This morning when I was set free from jail I thought I would probably starve, and here I am on my way to California to dig gold."

Yes, it was Lem, our hero, talking. He was sitting in the dining room of the "Fifth Avenue Special" *en route* to Chicago, where he and the party he was traveling with were to change to "The Chief," crack train of the Atchison, Topeka and Santa Fe, and continue on to the high Sierras.

With him in the dining room were Betty, Mr. Whipple and Jake Raven, and the four friends were in a cheerful mood as they ate the excellent food provided by the Pullman Company.

The explanation of how this had come about is quite simple. While Lem and Betty were warming themselves in the waiting room of the Grand Central Station, they had spied Mr. Whipple on line at one of the ticket booths. Lem had approached the ex-banker and had been greeted effusively by him, for he was indeed glad to see the boy. He was also glad to see Betty, whose father he had known before Mr. Prail's death in the fire.

After listening to Lem's account of the difficulties the two of them were in, he invited them to accompany him on his trip to California. It seemed that Mr. Whipple was going there with Jake Raven to dig gold from a mine that the redskin owned. With this money, he intended to finance the further activities of the National Revolutionary Party.

Lem was to help Mr. Whipple in the digging operations, while Betty was to keep house for the miners. The two young people jumped at this opportunity, as we can well imagine, and overwhelmed Mr. Whipple with their gratitude.

"In Chicago," said Shagpoke, when the dining car waiter had brought coffee, "we will have three hours and a half before 'The Chief' leaves for the Golden West. During that time, Lem, of course, will have to get himself a new set of store teeth and an eye, but I believe that the rest of us will still have time to pay a short visit to the World's Fair."

Mr. Whipple went on to describe the purpose of the fair, until, on a courteous signal from the head waiter, the little party was forced to leave their table and retire to their berths.

In the morning, when the train pulled into the depot, they disembarked. Lem was given some money to purchase the things he needed, while the others started immediately for the fair. He was to look for them on the grounds, if he got through in time.

Lem hurried as much as he could and managed quickly to select an eye and a set of teeth in a store devoted to that type of equipment. He then set out for the fair grounds.

As he was walking down Eleventh Street towards the North Entrance, he was accosted by a short, stout man, who wore a soft, black felt hat, the brim of which was slouched over his eyes. A full, brown beard concealed the lower part of his face.

"Excuse me," he said in a repressed tone of voice, "but I think you are the young man I am looking for."

"How is that?" asked Lem, instantly on his guard, for he did not intend to be snared by a sharper.

"Your name is Lemuel Pitkin, is it not?"

"It is, sir."

"I thought you answered the description given me."

"Given you by whom?" queried our hero.

"By Mr. Whipple, of course," was the surprising answer the stranger made.

"Why should he have given you a description of me?"

"So I could find you at the fair."

"But why, when I am to meet him at the depot in two hours from now?"

"An unfortunate accident has made it impossible for him to be there."

"An accident?"

"Exactly."

"What kind of an accident?"

"A very serious one, I am afraid. He was struck by a sightseeing bus and . . ."

"Killed!" cried Lem in dismay. "Tell me the truth, was he killed?"

"No, not exactly, but he was seriously injured, perhaps fatally. He was taken unconscious to a hospital. When he regained his senses, he asked for you and I was sent to fetch you to him. Miss Prail and Chief Raven are at his bedside."

Lem was so stunned by the dire news that it required some five minutes for him to recover sufficiently to gasp, "This is terrible!"

He asked the bearded stranger to take him to Mr. Whipple at once.

This was just what the man had counted on. "I have a car with me," he said with a bow. "Please enter it."

He then led our hero to a powerful limousine that was drawn up at the curb. Lem got in, and the chauffeur, who was wearing green goggles and a long linen duster, drove off at top speed.

All this seemed natural to the lad because of his agitated state of mind, and the rate at which the car traveled pleased him rather than otherwise, for he was anxious to get to Mr. Whipple's bedside.

The limousine passed rapidly under one elevated structure and then another. There were fruit vendors on the street corners and merchants peddling neckties. People moved to and fro on the sidewalks; cabs, trucks and private vehicles flitted past. The roar of the great city rose on every side, but Lem saw and heard nothing.

"Where was Mr. Whipple taken?" he asked presently.

"To the Lake Shore Hospital."

"And is this the quickest way there?"

"Most certainly."

With this the stranger lapsed into moody silence again.

Lem looked from the window of the limousine and saw that the cars and trucks were growing less in number. Soon they disappeared from the streets altogether. The people also became fewer till no more than an occasional pedestrian was to be observed and then only of the lowest type.

As the car approached an extremely disreputable neighborhood, the bearded stranger drew the shade of one of its two windows.

"Why did you do that?" demanded Lem.

"Because the sun hurts my eyes," he said as he deliberately drew the other shade, throwing the interior into complete darkness.

These acts made Lem think that all was not quite as it should be.

"I must have one or both of these shades up," he said, reaching for the nearest one to raise it.

"And I say that they must both remain down," returned the man in a low harsh voice.

"What do you mean, sir?"

A strong hand suddenly fastened in a grip of iron on Lem's throat, and these words reached his ears:

"I mean, Lemuel Pitkin, that you are in the power of the Third International."

23

Although thus suddenly attacked, Lem grappled with his assailant, determined to sell his life as dearly as possible.

The lad had been one of the best athletes in the Ottsville High School, and when aroused he was no mean adversary, as the bearded man soon discovered. He tore at the hand which was strangling him and succeeded in removing it from his throat, but when he tried to cry out for help, he discovered that the terrible pressure had robbed him of his vocal powers.

Even if he had been able to cry out it would have been useless for him to do so because the chauffeur was in the plot. Without once looking behind, he stepped on his accelerator and turned sharply into a noisome, dark alley.

Lem struck out savagely and landed a stiff blow in his opponent's face. That worthy uttered a fierce imprecation but did not strike back. He was fumbling for something in his pocket.

Lem struck again, and this time his hand caught in

the beard. It proved to be false and came away readily.

Although it was dark in the car, if you had been sitting in it, dear reader, you would have recognized our hero's assailant to be none other than the fat man in the Chesterfield overcoat. Lem, however, did not recognize him because he had never seen him before.

Suddenly, as he battled with the stranger, he felt something cold and hard against his forehead. It was a pistol.

"Now, you fascist whelp, I have you! If you so much as move a finger, I'll blow you to hell!"

These words were not spoken; they were snarled.

"What do you want of me?" Lem managed to gasp.

"You were going to dig gold with Mr. Whipple. Where is the mine located?"

"I don't know," said Lem, speaking the truth, for Shagpoke had kept secret their final destination.

"You do know, you damned bourgeois. Tell me or . . ."

He was interrupted by the wild scream of a siren. The car swerved and bucked wildly, then there was a terrific crash. Lem felt as though he were being whirled rapidly through a dark tunnel full of clanging bells. Everything went black, and the last thing he was conscious of was a sharp, stabbing pain in his left hand.

When the poor lad recovered consciousness, he found himself stretched out upon a sort of a cot and he realized that he was still being carried somewhere. Near his head sat a man in a white suit, who was calmly smoking a cigar. Lem knew he was no longer in the limousine, for he saw that the rear end of the conveyance was wide open and admitted a great deal of light and air.

"What happened?" he asked naturally enough.

"So you are coming around. eh?" said the man in the white suit. "Well, I guess you will get well all right."

"But what happened?"

"You were in a bad smash-up."

"A smash-up? . . . Where are you taking me?"

"Don't get excited and I'll answer your questions. The limousine in which you were riding was struck by a fire engine and demolished. The driver must have run off, for you were the only one we found at the wreck. This is the ambulance of the Lake Shore Hospital and you are being taken there."

Lem now understood what he had been through, and thanked God that he was still alive.

"I hope you are not a violinist," the interne added mysteriously.

"No, I don't play, but why?"

"Because your left hand was badly mangled and I had to remove a part of it. The thumb, to be explicit."

Lem sighed deeply, but being a brave lad he forced himself to think of other things.

"What hospital is this ambulance from did you say?"

"The Lake Shore."

"Do you know how a patient called Nathan Whipple is getting on? He was run over on the fair grounds by a sightseeing bus."

"We have no patient by that name."

"Are you certain?"

"Absolutely. I know every accident case in the hospital."

Of a sudden everything became clear to Lem. "Then he tricked me with a lie!" he cried.

"Who did?" asked the interne.

Lem ignored his question. "What time is it?" he demanded.

"One o'clock."

"I have still fifteen minutes to make the train. Stop and let me off, please."

The ambulance doctor stared at our hero and wondered if the lad had gone crazy.

"I must get off," repeated Lem frantically.

"As a private citizen you of course can do as you like, but I advise you to go to the hospital."

"No," said Lem, "please, I must get to the depot at once. I have to catch a train."

"Well, I certainly admire your pluck. By George, I have half a mind to help you."

"Do," begged Lem.

Without further argument, the interne told his driver to head for the depot at top speed and to ignore all traffic laws. After an exciting ride through the city, they arrived at their destination just as "The Chief" was about to pull out.

24

As Lem had suspected, Mr. Whipple and his other friends were safe on the train. When they saw his bandaged hand, they demanded an explanation and the poor lad told the story of his adventure with the agent of the Third International. They were astounded and angered, as well they might be.

"One day," Mr. Whipple said ominously, "heads will roll in the sand, bearded and unbearded alike."

The rest of the trip proved uneventful. There happened to be an excellent doctor on board and he had our hero's hand in fair shape by the time the train reached southern California.

After several days of travel on horseback, the little party arrived at the Yuba River in the high Sierra Mountains. It was on one of the tributaries of this river that Jake Raven's gold mine was located.

Next to the diggings was a log cabin, which the men of the party soon had in a livable condition. Mr. Whipple and Betty occupied it, while Lem and the redskin made their bed under the stars.

One evening, after a hard day's work at the mine, the four friends were sitting around a fire drinking coffee when a man appeared who might have sat for the photograph of a Western bad man without any alteration in his countenance or apparel.

He wore a red flannel shirt, pants of leather with the hair still on them and a Mexican sombrero. He had a bowie knife in his boot and displayed two pearl-handled revolvers very ostentatiously.

When he was about two rods away from the group, he hailed it.

"How are you, strangers?" he asked.

"Pretty comfortable," said Shagpoke. "How fare you?"

"You're a Yank, ain't you?" he asked as he dismounted from his horse.

"Yes, from Vermont. Where might your home be?"

"I'm from Pike County, Missouri," was the answer. "You've heard of Pike, hain't you?"

"I've heard of Missouri," said Mr. Whipple with a smile, "but I can't say as I ever heard of your particular county."

The man with the leather pants frowned.

"You must have been born in the woods not to have heard of Pike County," he said. "The smartest fighters come from there. I kin whip my weight in wildcats, am a match for a dozen Injuns to oncet, and can tackle a lion without flinchin'."

"Won't you stop and rest with us?" said Mr. Whipple politely.

"I don't care if I do," was the uncouth Missourian's rejoinder. "You don't happen to have a bottle of whisky with you, strangers?" he asked.

"No," said Lem.

The newcomer looked disappointed.

"I wish you had," he said. "I feel dry as a salt herring. What are you doing here?"

"Mining," said Mr. Whipple.

"Grubbin' in the ground," said the stranger with disgust. "That's no job for a gentleman."

This last was uttered in such a magnificent tone of disdain that everyone smiled. In his red shirt, coarse leather breeches and brown, not overclean skin, he certainly didn't look much like a gentleman in the conventional sense of the term.

"It's well enough to be a gentleman, if you've got money to fall back on," remarked Lem sensibly but not offensively.

"Is that personal?" demanded the Pike County man, scowling and half rising from the ground.

"It's personal to me," said Lem quietly.

"I accept the apology," said the Missourian fiercely. "But you'd better not rile me, stranger, for I'm powerful bad. You don't know me, you don't. I'm a rip-tail roarer and a ring-tail squealer, I am. I always kills the man what riles me."

After this last bloodthirsty declaration, the man from Pike County temporarily subsided. He partook quietly of the coffee and cake which Betty served him. Suddenly he flared up again.

"Hain't that an Injun?" he shouted, pointing at Jake Raven and reaching for his gun.

Lem stepped hastily in front of the redskin, while Shagpoke grabbed the ruffian's wrist.

"He's a good friend of ours," said Betty.

"I don't give a darn," said the ring-tail squealer. "Turn me loose and I'll massacree the danged aboriginee."

Jake Raven, however, could take care of himself. He pulled his own revolver and pointing it at the bad man said, "Rascal shut up or me kill um pronto quick."

At the sight of the Indian's drawn gun, the ruffian calmed down.

"All right," he said, "but it's my policy always to shoot

an Injun on sight. The only good Injun is a dead one, is what I alluz say."

Mr. Whipple sent Jake Raven away from the fire and there was a long silence, during which everyone stared at the cheery flames. Finally the man from Pike County again broke into speech, this time addressing Lem.

"How about a game of cards, sport?" he asked. With these words he drew a greasy pack out of his pocket and shuffled them with great skill.

"I have never played cards in my life," said our hero.

"Where was you raised?" demanded the Missourian contemptuously.

"Ottsville, State of Vermont," said Lem. "I don't know one card from another, and don't want to know."

In no way abashed, the Pike man said, "I'll larn you. How about a game of poker?"

Mr. Whipple spoke up. "We do not permit gambling in this camp," he said firmly.

"That's durn foolishness," said the stranger, whose object it was to victimize his new friends, being an expert gambler.

"Perhaps it is," said Mr. Whipple. "But that's our business."

"Look here, hombre," blustered the bully. "I reckon you don't realize who you're a-talking to. 'Tarnal death and massacreeation, I'm the rip-tail roarer, I am."

"You told us that before," said Mr. Whipple quietly.

"Blood and massacreeation, if I don't mean it, too," exclaimed the Missourian with a fierce scowl. "Do you know how I treated a man last week?"

"No," said Mr. Whipple, truthfully.

"We was ridin' together over in Almeda County. We'd met permiscuous, like we've met tonight. I was tellin' him how four b'ars attacked me to oncet, and how I fit 'em all single-handed, when he laughed and said he reckoned

I'd been drinkin' and seed double. If he'd a-know'd me better he wouldn't have done it."

"What did you do?" asked Betty in horror.

"What did I do, madam?" echoed the Pike County man ferociously. "I told him he didn't realize who he'd insulted. I told him I was a ring-tail squealer and a rip-tail roarer. I told him that he had to fight, and asked him how it would be. Foot and fist, or tooth and nail, or claw and mudscraper, or knife, gun and tommyhawk."

"Did he fight?" asked Lem.

"He had to."

"How did it come out?"

"I shot him through the heart," said the Missourian coldly. "His bones are bleachin' in the canyon where he fell."

25

The next day, the Pike County man lay on his blankets until about eleven o'clock in the morning. He only got up when Lem, Jake and Shagpoke returned from their work on the creek to eat lunch. They were surprised to see him still in camp, but said nothing out of politeness.

Although they did not know it, the Missourian had not been sleeping. He had been lying under a tree, thinking dirty thoughts as he watched Betty go about her household chores.

"I'm hungry," he announced with great truculence. "When do we eat?"

"Won't you share our lunch?" asked Mr. Whipple with a sarcastic smile that was completely lost on the uncouth fellow.

"Thank ye, stranger, I don't mind if I do," the Pike County man said. "My fodder give out just before I made your camp, and I hain't found a place to stock up."

He displayed such an appetite that Mr. Whipple regarded him with anxiety. The camp was short of provisions,
and if the stranger kept eating like that he would have to
take a trip into town that very afternoon for more food.

"You have a healthy appetite, my friend," Mr. Whipple
said.

"I generally have," said the Pike man. "You'd orter keep
some whisky to wash these vittles down with."

"We prefer coffee," said Lem.

"Coffee is for children, whisky for strong men," was
the ring-tail squealer's rejoinder.

"I still prefer coffee," Lem said firmly.

"Bah!" said the other, disdainfully; "I'd as soon drink
skim milk. Good whisky or cawn for me."

"The only thing I miss in this camp," said Mr. Whipple,
"is baked beans and brown bread. Ever eat 'em, stranger?"

"No," said the Pike man, "none of your Yankee truck for
me."

"What's your favorite food?" asked Lem with a smile.

"Sow teats and hominy, hoe cakes and forty-rod."

"Well," said Lem, "it depends on how you've been
brought up. I like baked beans and brown bread and
pumpkin pie. Ever eat pumpkin pie?"

"Yes."

"Like it?"

"I don't lay much on it."

Throughout this dialogue, the stranger ate enormous
quantities of food and drank six or seven cups of coffee.
Mr. Whipple realized that the damage was done and that
he would have to go into the town of Yuba for a fresh
supply of provisions.

Having finished three cans of pineapple, the Pike man
became social over one of Mr. Whipple's cigars, which he
had taken without so much as a "by-your-leave."

"Strangers," he said, "did you ever hear of the affair I had with Jack Scott?"

"No," said Mr. Whipple.

"Jack and me used to be a heap together. We went huntin' together, camped out for weeks together, and was like two brothers. One day we was a-ridin' out, when a deer started up about fifty yards ahead of us. We both raised our guns and shot at him. There was only one bullet into him, and I knowed it was mine."

"How did you know it?" asked Lem.

"Don't you get curious, stranger. I knowed it, and that was enough. But Jack said it was his. 'It's my deer,' he says, 'for you missed your shot.' 'Looka here, Jack,' says I, 'you're mistaken. You missed it. Don't you think I know my own bullet?' 'No, I don't,' says he. 'Jack,' says I calmly, 'don't talk that way. It's dangerous.' 'Do you think I'm afraid of you?' he says turnin' on me. 'Jack,' says I, 'don't provoke me. I kin whip my weight in wildcats.' 'You can't whip me,' he says. That was too much for me to stand. I'm the rip-tail roarer from Pike County, Missouri, and no man can insult me and live. 'Jack,' says I, 'we've been friends, but you've insulted me and you must pay with your life.' Then I up with my iron and shot him through the head."

"My, how cruel!" exclaimed Betty.

"I was sorry to do it, beautiful gal, for he was my best friend, but he disputed my word, and the man that does that has to make his will if he's got property."

No one said anything, so the Pike man continued to talk.

"You see," he said with a friendly smile. "I was brought up on fightin'. When I was a boy I could whip every boy in the school."

"That's why they call you a rip-tail roarer," said Mr. Whipple jokingly.

"You're right, pardner," said the Pike man complacently.

"What did you do when the teacher gave you a licking?" asked Mr. Whipple.

"What did I do?" yelled the Missourian with a demoniac laugh.

"Yes, what?" asked Mr. Whipple.

"Why, I shot him dead," said the Pike man briefly.

"My," said Mr. Whipple with a smile. "How many teachers did you shoot when you were a boy?"

"Only one. The rest heard of it and never dared touch me."

After this last statement, the desperado lay down under a tree to finish in comfort the cigar he had snatched from Mr. Whipple.

Seeing that he did not intend to move just yet, the others proceeded to go about their business. Lem and Jake Raven went to the mine, which was about a mile from the cabin. Shagpoke saddled his horse for the ride into town after a fresh stock of provisions. Betty occupied herself over the washtub.

Some time had elapsed, when Lem and Jake Raven decided that they would need dynamite to continue their operations. Lem was down at the bottom of the shaft, so the Indian was the one to go to camp for the explosives.

When Jake did not return after several hours, Lem began to worry about him. He remembered what the Pike man had said about his Indian policy and was afraid that that ruffian might have done Jake an injury.

Our hero decided to go back and see if everything was all right. When he entered the clearing in which the cabin stood, he was surprised to find the place deserted.

"Hi, Jake!" Lem shouted bewilderedly. "Hi, Jake Raven!"

There was no answer. Only the woods sent his words back to him in an echo almost as loud as his shout.

Suddenly, a scream rent the silence. Lem recognized the

voice of the screamer as Betty's, and ran quickly toward the cabin.

26

The door was locked. Lem hammered on it, but no one answered. He went to the woodpile to get an ax and there found Jake Raven lying on the ground. He had been shot through the chest. Hastily snatching up the ax Lem ran to the cabin. A few hearty blows and the door tumbled in.

In the half gloom of the cabin, Lem was horrified to see the Pike man busily tearing off Betty's sole remaining piece of underwear. She was struggling as best she could, but the ruffian from Missouri was too strong for her.

Lem raised the ax high over his head and started forward to interfere. He did not get very far because the ruffian had prepared for just such a contingency by setting an enormous bear trap inside the door.

Our hero stepped on the pan of the trap and its saw-toothed jaws closed with great force on the calf of his leg, cutting through his trousers, skin, flesh and halfway into the bone besides. He dropped in a heap, as though he had been shot through the brain.

At the sight of poor Lem weltering in his own blood, Betty fainted. In no way disturbed, the Missourian went coolly about his nefarious business and soon accomplished his purpose.

With the hapless girl in his arms he then left the cabin. Throwing her behind his saddle, he pressed his cruel spurs into his horse's sides and galloped off in the general direction of Mexico.

Once more the deep hush of the primeval forest descended on the little clearing, making peaceful what had been a scene of wild torment and savage villainy. A squirrel began to chatter hysterically in a treetop and from somewhere along the brook came the plash of a rising trout. Birds sang.

Suddenly the birds were still. The squirrel fled from the tree in which he had been gathering pine cones. Something was moving behind the woodpile. Jake Raven was not dead after all.

With all the stoical disregard of pain for which his race is famous, the sorely wounded Indian crawled along on his hands and knees. His progress was slow but sure.

Some three miles away was the boundary line of the California Indian Reservation. Jake knew that there was an encampment of his people close by the line and it was to them that he was going for help.

After a long, tortuous struggle, he arrived at his destination, but his efforts had so weakened him that he fainted dead away in the arms of the first redskin to reach him. Not before, however, he had managed to mumble the following words:

"White man shoot. Go camp quick. . . ."

Leaving Jake to the tender ministrations of the village squaws, the warriors of the tribe assembled around the wigwam of their chief to plan a course of action. Somewhere a tom-tom began to throb.

The chief's name was Israel Satinpenny. He had been to Harvard and hated the white man with undying venom. For many years now, he had been trying to get the Indian nations to rise and drive the palefaces back to the countries from which they had come, but so far he had had little success. His people had grown soft and lost their warlike ways. Perhaps, with the wanton wounding of Jake Raven, his chance had come.

When the warriors had all gathered around his tent, he appeared in full regalia and began a harangue.

"Red men!" he thundered. "The time has come to protest

in the name of the Indian peoples and to cry out against that abomination of abominations, the paleface.

"In our father's memory this was a fair, sweet land, where a man could hear his heart beat without wondering if what he heard wasn't an alarm clock, where a man could fill his nose with pleasant flower odors without finding that they came from a bottle. Need I speak of springs that had never known the tyranny of iron pipes? Of deer that had never tasted hay? Of wild ducks that had never been banded by the U.S. Department of Conservation?

"In return for the loss of these things, we accepted the white man's civilization, syphilis and the radio, tuberculosis and the cinema. We accepted his civilization because he himself believed in it. But now that he has begun to doubt, why should we continue to accept? His final gift to us is doubt, a soul-corroding doubt. He rotted this land in the name of progress, and now it is he himself who is rotting. The stench of his fear stinks in the nostrils of the great god Manitou.

"In what way is the white man wiser than the red? We lived here from time immemorial and everything was sweet and fresh. The paleface came and in his wisdom filled the sky with smoke and the rivers with refuse. What, in his wisdom, was he doing? I'll tell you. He was making clever cigarette lighters. He was making superb fountain pens. He was making paper bags, doorknobs, leatherette satchels. All the powers of water, air and earth he made to turn his wheels within wheels within wheels within wheels. They turned, sure enough, and the land was flooded with toilet paper, painted boxes to keep pins in, key rings, watch fobs, leatherette satchels.

"When the paleface controlled the things he manufactured, we red men could only wonder at and praise his ability to hide his vomit. But now all the secret places of the earth are full. Now even the Grand Canyon will no longer hold razor blades. Now the dam, O warriors, has broken and he is up to his neck in the articles of his manufacture.

"He has loused the continent up good. But is he trying to de-louse it? No, all his efforts go to keep on lousing up the joint. All that worries him is how he can go on making little painted boxes for pins, watch fobs, leatherette satchels.

"Don't mistake me, Indians. I'm no Rousseauistic philosopher. I know that you can't put the clock back. But there is one thing you can do. You can stop that clock. You can smash that clock.

"The time is ripe. Riot and profaneness, poverty and violence are everywhere. The gates of pandemonium are open and through the land stalk the gods Mapeeo and Suraniou.

"The day of vengeance is here. The star of the paleface is sinking and he knows it. Spengler has said so; Valéry has said so; thousands of his wise men proclaim it.

"O, brothers, this is the time to run upon his neck and the bosses of his armor. While he is sick and fainting, while he is dying of a surfeit of shoddy."

Wild yells for vengeance broke from the throats of the warriors. Shouting their new war cry of "Smash that clock!" they smeared themselves with bright paint and mounted their ponies. In every brave's hand was a tomahawk and between his teeth a scalping knife.

Before jumping on his own mustang, Chief Satinpenny ordered one of his lieutenants to the nearest telegraph office. From there he was to send code messages to all the Indian tribes in the United States, Canada and Mexico, ordering them to rise and slay.

With Satinpenny leading them, the warriors galloped

through the forest over the trail that Jake Raven had come. When they arrived at the cabin, they found Lem still fast in the unrelenting jaws of the bear trap.

"Yeehoieee!" screamed the chief, as he stooped over the recumbent form of the poor lad and tore the scalp from his head. Then brandishing his reeking trophy on high, he sprang on his pony and made for the nearest settlements, followed by his horde of blood-crazed savages.

An Indian boy remained behind with instructions to fire the cabin. Fortunately, he had no matches and tried to do it with two sticks, but no matter how hard he rubbed them together he alone grew warm.

With a curse unbecoming one of his few years, he left off to go swimming in the creek, first looting Lem's bloody head of its store teeth and glass eye.

27

A few hours later, Mr. Whipple rode on the scene with his load of provisions. The moment he entered the clearing he knew that something was wrong and hurried to the cabin. There he found Lem with his leg still in the bear trap.

He bent over the unconscious form of the poor, mutilated lad and was happy to discover that his heart still beat. He tried desperately to release the trap, but failed, and was forced to carry Lem out of the cabin with it dangling from his leg.

Placing our hero across the pommel of his saddle, he galloped all that night, arriving at the county hospital the next morning. Lem was immediately admitted to the ward, where the good doctors began their long fight to save the lad's life. They triumphed, but not before they had found it necessary to remove his leg at the knee.

With the disappearance of Jake Raven, there was no use in Mr. Whipple's returning to the mine, so he remained near Lem, visiting the poor boy every day. Once he brought him an orange to eat, another time some simple wild flowers which he himself had gathered.

Lem's convalescence was a long one. Before it was over all of Shagpoke's funds were spent, and the ex-President was forced to work in a livery stable in order to keep body and soul together. When our hero left the hospital, he joined him there.

At first Lem had some difficulty in using the wooden leg with which the hospital authorities had equipped him. Practice, however, makes perfect, and in time he was able to help Mr. Whipple clean the stalls and curry the horses.

It goes without saying that the two friends were not satisfied to remain hostlers. They both searched for more suitable employment, but there was none to be had.

Shagpoke's mind was quick and fertile. One day, as he watched Lem show his scalped skull for the twentieth time, he was struck by an idea. Why not get a tent and exhibit his young friend as the last man to have been scalped by the Indians and the sole survivor of the Yuba River massacre?

Our hero was not very enthusiastic about the plan, but Mr. Whipple finally managed to convince him that it was the only way in which they could hope to escape from their drudgery in the livery stable. He promised Lem that as soon as they had accumulated a little money they would abandon the tent show and enter some other business.

Out of an old piece of tarpaulin they fashioned a rough tent. Mr. Whipple then obtained a crate of cheap kerosene lighters from a dealer in pedlar's supplies. With this meager equipment they took to the open road.

Their method of work was very simple. When they arrived at the outskirts of a likely town, they set up their tent. Lem hid himself inside it, while Mr. Whipple beat furiously on the bottom of a tin can with a stick.

In a short while, he was surrounded by a crowd eager to know what the noise was about. After describing the merits of his kerosene lighters, he made his audience a "dual" offer. For the same ten cents, they could both obtain a cigarette lighter and enter the tent where they would see the sole survivor of the Yuba River massacre, getting a close view of his freshly scalped skull.

Business was not as good as they had thought it would be. Although Mr. Whipple was an excellent salesman, the people they encountered had very little money to spend and could not afford to gratify their curiosity no matter how much it was aroused.

One day, after many weary months on the road, the two friends were about to set up their tent, when a small boy volunteered the information that there was a much bigger show being given free at the local opera house. Realizing that it would be futile for them to try to compete with this other attraction, they decided to visit it.

There were bills posted on every fence, and the two friends stopped to read one of them.

FREE   FREE   FREE
Chamber of American Horrors
Animate and Inanimate
Hideosities
also
Chief Jake Raven
COME ONE   COME ALL
S. Snodgrasse
Mgr.
FREE   FREE   FREE

Delighted to discover that their red-skinned friend was still alive, they set out to find him. He was coming down the steps of the opera house just as they arrived there, and his joy on seeing them was very great. He insisted on their accompanying him to a restaurant.

Over his coffee, Jake explained that after being shot by the man from Pike County, he had crawled to the Indian encampment. There his wounds had been healed by the use of certain medicaments secret to the squaws of his tribe. It was this same elixir that he was now selling in conjunction with the "Chamber of American Horrors."

Lem in his turn told how he had been scalped and how Mr. Whipple had arrived just in time to carry him to the hospital. After listening sympathetically to the lad's story, Jake expressed his anger in no uncertain terms. He condemned Chief Satinpenny for being a hothead, and assured Lem and Mr. Whipple that the respectable members of the tribe frowned on Satinpenny's activities.

Although Mr. Whipple believed Jake, he was not satisfied that the Indian rising was as simple as it seemed. "Where," he asked the friendly redskin, "had Satinpenny obtained the machine guns and whisky needed to keep his warriors in the field?"

Jake was unable to answer this question, and Mr. Whipple smiled as though he knew a great deal more than he was prepared to divulge at this time.

28

"I remember your administration very well," said Sylvanus Snodgrasse to Mr. Whipple. "It will be an honor to have you and your young friend, whom I also know and admire, in my employ."

"Thank you," said both Shagpoke and Lem together.

"You will spend today rehearsing your roles and tomorrow you will appear in the pageant."

It was through the good offices of Jake Raven that the above interview was made possible. Realizing how poor they were, he had suggested that the two friends abandon their own little show and obtain positions in the one with which he was traveling.

As soon as Shagpoke and Lem left the manager's office, an inner door opened and through it entered a certain man. If they had seen him and had known who he was, they would have been greatly surprised. Moreover, they would not have been quite so happy over their new jobs.

This stranger was none other than the fat man in the Chesterfield overcoat, Operative 6348XM, or Comrade Z as he was known at a different address. His presence in Snodgrasse's office is explained by the fact that the "Chamber of American Horrors, Animate and Inanimate Hideosities," although it appeared to be a museum, was in reality a bureau for disseminating propaganda of the most subversive nature. It had been created and financed to this end by the same groups that employed the fat man.

Snodgrasse had become one of their agents because of his inability to sell his "poems." Like many another "poet," he blamed his literary failure on the American public instead of on his own lack of talent, and his desire for revolution was really a desire for revenge. Furthermore, having lost faith in himself, he thought it his duty to undermine the nation's faith in itself.

As its name promised, the show was divided into two parts, "animate" and "inanimate." Let us first briefly consider the latter, which consisted of innumerable objects culled from the popular art of the country and of an equally large number of manufactured articles of the kind detested so heartily by Chief Satinpenny.

("Can this be a coincidence?" Mr. Whipple was later to ask.)

The hall which led to the main room of the "inanimate" exhibit was lined with sculptures in plaster. Among the most striking of these was a Venus de Milo with a clock in her abdomen, a copy of Power's "Greek Slave" with elastic bandages on all her joints, A Hercules wearing a small, compact truss.

In the center of the principal salon was a gigantic hemorrhoid that was lit from within by electric lights. To give the effect of throbbing pain, these lights went on and off.

All was not medical, however. Along the walls were tables on which were displayed collections of objects whose distinction lay in the great skill with which their materials had been disguised. Paper had been made to look like wood, wood like rubber, rubber like steel, steel like cheese, cheese like glass, and, finally, glass like paper.

Other tables carried instruments whose purposes were dual and sometimes triple or even sextuple. Among the most ingenious were pencil sharpeners that could also be used as earpicks, can openers as hair brushes. Then, too, there was a large variety of objects whose real uses had been cleverly camouflaged. The visitor saw flower pots that were really victrolas, revolvers that held candy, candy that held collar buttons and so forth.

The "animate" part of the show took place in the auditorium of the opera house. It was called "The Pageant of America or A Curse on Columbus," and consisted of a series of short sketches in which Quakers were shown being branded, Indians brutalized and cheated, Negroes sold, children sweated to death. Snodgrasse tried to make obvious the relationship between these sketches and the "inanimate" exhibit by a little speech in which he claimed that the former had resulted in the latter. His arguments were not very convincing, however.

The "pageant" culminated in a small playlet which I will attempt to set down from memory. When the curtain rises, the audience sees the comfortable parlor of a typical American home. An old, white-haired grandmother is knitting near the fire while the three small sons of her dead daughter play together on the floor. From a radio in the corner comes a rich, melodic voice.

Radio: "The Indefatigable Investment Company of Wall Street wishes its unseen audience all happiness, health and wealth, especially the latter. Widows, orphans, cripples, are you getting a large enough return on your capital? Is the money left by your departed ones bringing you all that they desired you to have in the way of comforts? Write or telephone . . ."

Here the stage becomes dark for a few seconds. When the lights are bright again, we hear the same voice, but see that this time it comes from a sleek, young salesman. He is talking to the old grandmother. The impression given is that of a snake and a bird. The old lady is the bird, of course.

Sleek Salesman: "Dear Madam, in South America lies the fair, fertile land of Iguania. It is a marvelous country, rich in minerals and oil. For five thousand dollars—yes, Madam, I'm advising you to sell all your Liberty Bonds —you will get ten of our Gold Iguanians, which yield seventeen per centum per annum. These bonds are secured by a first mortgage on all the natural resources of Iguania."

Grandmother: "But I . . ."

Sleek Salesman: "You will have to act fast, as we have only a limited number of Gold Iguanians left. The ones I am offering you are part of a series set aside by our company especially for widows and orphans. It was necessary for us to do this because otherwise the big banks and mortgage companies would have snatched up the entire issue."

Grandmother: "But I . . ."

The Three Small Sons: "Goo, goo. . . ."

Sleek Salesman: "Think of these kiddies, Madam. Soon they will be ready for college. They will want Brooks suits and banjos and fur coats like the other boys. How will you feel when you have to refuse them these things because of your stubbornness?"

Here the curtain falls for a change of scene. It rises again on a busy street. The old grandmother is seen lying in the gutter with her head pillowed against the curb. Around her are arranged her three grandchildren, all very evidently dead of starvation.

Grandmother (feebly to the people who hurry past): "We are starving. Bread . . . bread . . ."

No one pays any attention to her and she dies.

An idle breeze plays mischievously with the rags draping the four corpses. Suddenly it whirls aloft several sheets of highly engraved paper, one of which is blown across the path of two gentlemen in silk hats, on whose vests huge dollar signs are embroidered. They are evidently millionaires.

First Millionaire (picking up engraved paper): "Hey, Bill, isn't this one of your Iguanian Gold Bonds?" (He laughs.)

Second Millionaire (echoing his companion's laughter): "Sure enough. That's from the special issue for widows and orphans. I got them out in 1928 and they sold like hot cakes. (He turns the bond over in his hands, admiring it.) I'll tell you one thing, George, it certainly pays to do a good printing job."

Laughing heartily, the two millionaires move along the street. In their way lie the four dead bodies and they almost trip over them. They exit cursing the street cleaning department for its negligence.

29

The "Chamber of American Horrors, Animate and Inanimate Hideosities," reached Detroit about a month after the two friends had joined it. It was while they were playing there that Lem questioned Mr. Whipple about the show. He was especially disturbed by the scene in which the millionaires stepped on the dead children.

"In the first place," Mr. Whipple said, in reply to Lem's questions, "the grandmother didn't have to buy the bonds unless she wanted to. Secondly, the whole piece is made ridiculous by the fact that no one can die in the streets. The authorities won't stand for it."

"But," said Lem, "I thought you were against the capitalists?"

"Not all capitalists," answered Shagpoke. "The distinction must be made between bad capitalists and good capitalists, between the parasites and the creators. I am against the parasitical international bankers, but not the creative American capitalists, like Henry Ford for example."

"Are not capitalists who step on the faces of dead children bad?"

"Even if they are," replied Shagpoke, "it is very wrong to show the public scenes of that sort. I object to them because they tend to foment bad feeling between the classes."

"I see," said Lem.

"What I am getting at," Mr. Whipple went on, "is that Capital and Labor must be taught to work together for the general good of the country. Both must be made to drop the materialistic struggle for higher wages on the one hand and bigger profits on the other. Both must be made to realize that the only struggle worthy of Americans is the idealistic one of their country against its enemies, England, Japan, Russia, Rome and Jerusalem. Always remember, my boy, that class war is civil war, and will destroy us."

"Shouldn't we then try to dissuade Mr. Snodgrasse from continuing with his show?" asked Lem innocently.

"No," replied Shagpoke. "If we try to he will merely get rid of us. Rather must we bide our time until a good opportunity presents itself, then denounce him for what he is, and his show likewise. Here, in Detroit, there are too many Jews, Catholics and members of unions. Unless I am greatly mistaken, however, we will shortly turn south. When we get to some really American town, we will act."

Mr. Whipple was right in his surmise. After playing a few more Midwestern cities, Snodgrasse headed his company south along the Mississippi River, finally arriving in the town of Beulah for a one-night stand.

"Now is the time for us to act," announced Mr. Whipple in a hoarse whisper to Lem, when he had obtained a good look at the inhabitants of Beulah. "Follow me."

Our hero accompanied Shagpoke to the town barber shop, which was run by one Keely Jefferson, a fervent Southerner of the old school. Mr. Whipple took the master barber to one side. After a whispered colloquy, he agreed to arrange a meeting of the town's citizens for Shagpoke to address.

By five o'clock that same evening, all the inhabitants of Beulah who were not colored, Jewish or Catholic assembled under a famous tree from whose every branch a Negro had dangled at one time or other. They stood together, almost a thousand strong, drinking Coca-Colas and joking with their friends. Although every third citizen carried either a rope or a gun, their cheerful manner belied the seriousness of the occasion.

Mr. Jefferson mounted a box to introduce Mr. Whipple.

"Fellow townsmen, Southerners, Protestants, Americans," he began. "You have been called here to listen to the words of Shagpoke Whipple, one of the few Yanks whom we of the South can trust and respect. He ain't no nigger-lover, he don't give a damn for Jewish culture, and he knows the fine Italian hand of the Pope when he sees it. Mr. Whipple . . ."

Shagpoke mounted the box which Mr. Jefferson vacated and waited for the cheering to subside. He began by placing his hand on his heart. "I love the South," he announced. "I love her because her women are beautiful and chaste, her men brave and gallant, and her fields warm and fruitful. But there is one thing that I love more than the South . . . my country, these United States."

The cheers which greeted this avowal were even wilder and hoarser than those that had gone before it. Mr. Whipple held up his hand for silence, but it was fully five minutes before his audience would let him continue.

"Thank you," he cried happily, much moved by the enthusiasm of his hearers. "I know that your shouts rise from the bottom of your honest, fearless hearts. And I am grateful because I also know that you are cheering, not me, but the land we love so well.

"However, this is not a time or place for flowery speeches, this is a time for action. There is an enemy in our midst, who, by boring from within, undermines our institutions and threatens our freedom. Neither hot lead nor cold steel are his weapons, but insidious propaganda. He strives by it to set brother against brother, those who have not against those who have.

"You stand here now, under this heroic tree, like the free men that you are, but tomorrow you will become the slaves of Socialists and Bolsheviks. Your sweethearts and wives will become the common property of foreigners to maul and mouth at their leisure. Your shops will be torn from you and you will be driven from your farms. In return you will be thrown a stinking, slave's crust with Russian labels.

"Is the spirit of Jubal Early and Francis Marion then so dead that you can only crouch and howl like hound dogs? Have you forgotten Jefferson Davis?

"No?

"Then let those of you who remember your ancestors strike down Sylvanus Snodgrasse, that foul conspirator, that viper in the bosom of the body politic. Let those . . ."

Before Mr. Whipple had quite finished his little talk, the crowd ran off in all directions, shouting "Lynch him! Lynch him!" although a good three-quarters of its members did not know whom it was they were supposed to lynch. This fact did not bother them, however. They considered their lack of knowledge an advantage rather than a hindrance, for it gave them a great deal of leeway in their choice of a victim.

Those of the mob who were better informed made for the opera house where the "Chamber of American Horrors" was quartered. Snodgrasse, however, was nowhere to be found. He had been warned and had taken to his heels. Feeling that they ought to hang somebody, the crowd put a rope around Jake Raven's neck because of his dark complexion. They then fired the building.

Another section of Shagpoke's audience, made up mostly of older men, had somehow gotten the impression that the South had again seceded from the Union. Perhaps this had come about through their hearing Shagpoke mention the names of Jubal Early, Francis Marion and Jefferson Davis. They ran up the Confederate flag on the courthouse pole, and prepared to die in its defense.

Other, more practical-minded citizens proceeded to rob the bank and loot the principal stores, and to free all their relatives who had the misfortune to be in jail.

As time went on, the riot grew more general in character. Barricades were thrown up in the streets. The heads of Negroes were paraded on poles. A Jewish drummer was nailed to the door of his hotel room. The housekeeper of the local Catholic priest was raped.

30

Lem lost track of Mr. Whipple when the meeting broke up, and was unable to find him again although he searched everywhere. As he wandered around, he was shot at several times, and it was only by the greatest of good luck that he succeeded in escaping with his life.

He managed this by walking to the nearest town that had a depot and there taking the first train bound northeast. Unfortunately, all his money had been lost in the opera house fire and he was unable to pay for a ticket. The conductor, however, was a good-natured man. Seeing that the lad had only one leg, he waited until the train slowed down at a curve before throwing him off.

It was only a matter of twenty miles or so to the nearest highway, and Lem contrived to hobble there before dawn. Once on the highway, he was able to beg rides all the way to New York City, arriving there some ten weeks later.

Times had grown exceedingly hard with the inhabitants of that once prosperous metropolis and Lem's ragged, emaciated appearance caused no adverse comment. He

was able to submerge himself in the great army of unemployed.

Our hero differed from most of that army in several
ways, however. For one thing, he bathed regularly. Each
morning he took a cold plunge in the Central Park lake
on whose shores he was living in a piano crate. Also, he
visited daily all the employment agencies that were still
open, refusing to be discouraged or grow bitter and become a carping critic of things as they are.

One day, when he timidly opened the door of the
"Golden Gates Employment Bureau," he was greeted with
a welcoming smile instead of the usual jeers and curses.

"My boy," exclaimed Mr. Gates, the proprietor, "we
have obtained a position for you."

At this news, tears welled up in Lem's good eye and
his throat was so choked with emotion that he could not
speak.

Mr. Gates was surprised and nettled by the lad's silence,
not realizing its cause. "It's the opportunity of a lifetime,"
he said chidingly. "You have heard of course of the great
team of Riley and Robbins. They're billed wherever they
play as 'Fifteen Minutes of Furious Fun with Belly Laffs
Galore.' Well, Moe Riley is an old friend of mine. He
came in here this morning and asked me to get him a
'stooge' for his act. He wanted a one-eyed man, and the
minute he said that, I thought of you."

By now Lem had gained sufficient control over himself
to thank Mr. Gates, and he did so profusely.

"You almost didn't get the job," Mr. Gates went on,
when he had had enough of the mutilated boy's gratitude.
"There was a guy in here who heard Moe Riley talking to
me, and we had some time preventing him from poking
out one of his eyes so that he could qualify for the job.
We had to call a cop."

"Oh, that's too bad," said Lem sadly.

"But I told Riley that you also had a wooden leg, wore a toupee and store teeth, and he wouldn't think of hiring anybody but you."

When our hero reported to the Bijou Theater, where Riley and Robbins were playing, he was stopped at the stage door by the watchman, who was suspicious of his tattered clothes. He insisted on getting in, and the watchman finally agreed to take a message to the comedians. Soon afterwards, he was shown to their dressing room.

Lem stood in the doorway, fumbling with the piece of soiled cloth that served him as a cap, until the gales of laughter with which Riley and Robbins had greeted him subsided. Fortunately, it never struck the poor lad that he was the object of their merriment or he might have fled.

To be perfectly just, from a certain point of view, not a very civilized one it must be admitted, there was much to laugh at in our hero's appearance. Instead of merely having no hair like a man prematurely bald, the gray bone of his skull showed plainly where he had been scalped by Chief Satinpenny. Then, too, his wooden leg had been carved with initials, twined hearts and other innocent insignia by mischievous boys.

"You're a wow!" exclaimed the two comics in the argot of their profession. "You're a riot! You'll blow them out of the back of the house. Boy, oh boy, wait till the pus-pockets and fleapits get a load of you."

Although Lem did not understand their language, he was made exceedingly happy by the evident satisfaction he gave his employers. He thanked them effusively.

"Your salary will be twelve dollars a week," said Riley, who was the businessman of the team. "We wish we could pay you more, for you're worth more, but these are hard times in the theater."

Lem accepted without quibbling and they began at once

to rehearse him. His role was a simple one, with no spoken lines, and he was soon perfect in it. He made his debut on the stage that same night. When the curtain went up, he was discovered standing between the two comics and facing the audience. He was dressed in an old Prince Albert, many times too large for him, and his expression was one of extreme sobriety and dignity. At his feet was a large box the contents of which could not be seen by the audience.

Riley and Robbins wore striped blue flannel suits of the latest cut, white linen spats and pale gray derby hats. To accent further the contrast between themselves and their "stooge," they were very gay and lively. In their hands they carried newspapers rolled up into clubs.

As soon as the laughter caused by their appearance had died down, they began their "breezy crossfire of smart cracks."

Riley: "I say, my good man, who was that dame I saw you with last night?"

Robbins: "How could you see me last night? You were blind drunk."

Riley: "Hey, listen, you slob, that's not in the act and you know it."

Robbins: "Act? What act?"

Riley: "All right! All right! You're a great little kidder, but let's get down to business. I say to you: 'Who was that dame I saw you out with last night?' And you say: 'That was no dame, that was a damn.'"

Robbins: "So you're stealing my lines, eh?"

At this both actors turned on Lem and beat him violently over the head and body with their rolled-up newspapers. Their object was to knock off his toupee or to knock out his teeth and eye. When they had accomplished one or all of these goals, they stopped clubbing him. Then Lem, whose part it was not to move while he was being hit, bent over and with sober dignity took from the box at his feet, which contained a large assortment of false hair, teeth and eyes, whatever he needed to replace the things that had been knocked off or out.

The turn lasted about fifteen minutes and during this time Riley and Robbins told some twenty jokes, beating Lem ruthlessly at the end of each one. For a final curtain, they brought out an enormous wooden mallet labeled "The Works" and with it completely demolished our hero. His toupee flew off, his eye and teeth popped out, and his wooden leg was knocked into the audience.

At sight of the wooden leg, the presence of which they had not even suspected, the spectators were convulsed with joy. They laughed heartily until the curtain came down, and for some time afterwards.

Our hero's employers congratulated him on his success, and although he had a headache from their blows he was made quite happy by this. After all, he reasoned, with millions out of work he had no cause to complain.

One of Lem's duties was to purchase newspapers and out of them fashion the clubs used to beat him. When the performance was over, he was given the papers to read. They formed his only relaxation, for his meager salary made more complicated amusements impossible.

The mental reactions of the poor lad had been slowed up considerably by the hardships he had suffered, and it was a heart-rending sight to watch him as he bent over a paper to spell out the headlines. More than this he could not manage.

"PRESIDENT CLOSES BANKS FOR GOOD," he read one night. He sighed profoundly. Not because he had again lost the few dollars he had saved, which he had, but because it made him think of Mr. Whipple and the Rat River National Bank. He spent the rest of the night wondering what had become of his old friend.

Some weeks later he was to find out. "WHIPPLE DE-
MANDS DICTATORSHIP," he read. "LEATHER SHIRTS RIOT IN
SOUTH." Then, in rapid succession, came other headlines
announcing victories for Mr. Whipple's National Revolutionary Party. The South and West, Lem learned, were
solidly behind his movement and he was marching on
Chicago.

31

One day a stranger came to the theater to see Lem. He
addressed our hero as Commander Pitkin and said that he
was Storm Trooper Zachary Coates.

Lem made him welcome and asked eagerly for news of
Mr. Whipple. He was told that that very night Shagpoke
would be in the city. Mr. Coates then went on to explain
that because of its large foreign population New York was
still holding out against the National Revolutionary Party.

"But tonight," he said, "this city will be filled with
thousands of 'Leather Shirts' from upstate and an attempt
will be made to take it over."

While talking he stared hard at our hero. Apparently
satisfied with what he saw, he saluted briskly and said, "As
one of the original members of the party, you are being
asked to cooperate."

"I'll be glad to do anything I can to help," Lem replied.

"Good! Mr. Whipple will be happy to hear that, for he
counted on you."

"I am something of a cripple," Lem added with a brave
smile. "I may not be able to do much."

"We of the party know how your wounds were acquired.
In fact one of our prime purposes is to prevent the
youth of this country from being tortured as you were
tortured. Let me add, Commander Pitkin, that in my
humble opinion you are well on your way to being rec-

ognized as one of the martyrs of our cause." Here he saluted Lem once more.

Lem was embarrassed by the man's praise and hurriedly changed the subject. "What are Mr. Whipple's orders?" he asked.

"Tonight, wherever large crowds gather, in the parks, theaters, subways, a member of our party will make a speech. Scattered among his listeners will be numerous 'Leather Shirts' in plain clothes, who will aid the speaker stir up the patriotic fury of the crowd. When this fury reaches its proper height, a march on the City Hall will be ordered. There a monster mass meeting will be held which Mr. Whipple will address. He will demand and get control of the city."

"It sounds splendid," said Lem. "I suppose you want me to make a speech in this theater?"

"Yes, exactly."

"I would if I could," replied Lem, "but I'm afraid I can't. I have never made a speech in my life. You see, I'm not a real actor but only a 'stooge.' And besides, Riley and Robbins wouldn't like it if I tried to interrupt their act."

"Don't worry about those gentlemen." Mr. Coates said with a smile. "They will be taken care of. As for your other reason, I have a speech in my pocket that was written expressly for you by Mr. Whipple. I have come here to rehearse you in it."

Zachary Coates reached into his pocket and brought out a sheaf of papers. "Read this through first," he said firmly, "then we will begin to study it."

That night Lem walked out on the stage alone. Although he was not wearing his stage costume, but the dress uniform of the "Leather Shirts," the audience knew from the program that he was a comedian and roared with laughter.

This unexpected reception destroyed what little self-assurance the poor lad had and for a minute it looked as though he were going to run. Fortunately, however, the orchestra leader, who was a member of Mr. Whipple's organization, had his wits about him and made his men play the national anthem. The audience stopped laughing and rose soberly to its feet.

In all that multitude one man alone failed to stand up. He was our old friend, the fat fellow in the Chesterfield overcoat. Secreted behind the curtains of a box, he crouched low in his chair and fondled an automatic pistol. He was again wearing a false beard.

When the orchestra had finished playing, the audience reseated itself and Lem prepared to make his speech.

"I am a clown," he began, "but there are times when even clowns must grow serious. This is such a time. I . . ."

Lem got no further. A shot rang out and he fell dead, drilled through the heart by an assassin's bullet.

Little else remains to be told, but before closing this book there is one last scene which I must describe.

It is Pitkin's Birthday, a national holiday, and the youth of America is parading down Fifth Avenue in his honor. They are a hundred thousand strong. On every boy's head is a coonskin hat complete with jaunty tail, and on every shoulder rests a squirrel rifle.

Hear what they are singing. It is *The Lemuel Pitkin Song*.

"Who dares?"—this was L. Pitkin's cry,
   As striding on the Bijou stage he came—
"Surge out with me in Shagpoke's name,
   For him to live, for him to die!"
A million hands flung up reply,
A million voices answered, "I!"

Chorus

A million hearts for Pitkin, oh!
To do and die with Pitkin, oh!
To live and fight with Pitkin, oh!
Marching for Pitkin.

The youths pass the reviewing stand and from it Mr. Whipple proudly returns their salute. The years have dealt but lightly with him. His back is still as straight as ever and his gray eyes have not lost their keenness.

But who is the little lady in black next to the dictator? Can it be the Widow Pitkin? Yes, it is she. She is crying, for with a mother glory can never take the place of a beloved child. To her it seems like only yesterday that Lawyer Slemp threw Lem into the open cellar.

And next to the Widow Pitkin stands still another woman. This one is young and beautiful, yet her eyes too are full of tears. Let us look closer, for there is something vaguely familiar about her. It is Betty Prail. She seems to have some official position, and when we ask, a bystander tells us that she is Mr. Whipple's secretary.

The marchers have massed themselves in front of the reviewing stand and Mr. Whipple is going to address them.

"Why are we celebrating this day above other days?" he asked his hearers in a voice of thunder. "What made Lemuel Pitkin great? Let us examine his life.

"First we see him as a small boy, light of foot, fishing for bullheads in the Rat River of Vermont. Later, he attends the Ottsville High School, where he is captain of the nine and an excellent outfielder. Then, he leaves for the big city to make his fortune. All this is in the honorable tradition of his country and its people, and he has the right to expect certain rewards.

"Jail is his first reward. Poverty his second. Violence is his third. Death is his last.

"Simple was his pilgrimage and brief, yet a thousand years hence, no story, no tragedy, no epic poem will be filled with greater wonder, or be followed by mankind with deeper feeling, than that which tells of the life and death of Lemuel Pitkin.

"But I have not answered the question. Why is Lemuel Pitkin great? Why does the martyr move in triumph and the nation rise up at every stage of his coming? Why are cities and states his pallbearers?

"Because, although dead, yet he speaks.

"Of what is it that he speaks? Of the right of every American boy to go into the world and there receive fair play and a chance to make his fortune by industry and probity without being laughed at or conspired against by sophisticated aliens.

"Alas, Lemuel Pitkin himself did not have this chance, but instead was dismantled by the enemy. His teeth were pulled out. His eye was gouged from his head. His thumb was removed. His scalp was torn away. His leg was cut off. And, finally, he was shot through the heart.

"But he did not live or die in vain. Through his martyrdom the National Revolutionary Party triumphed, and by that triumph this country was delivered from sophistication, Marxism and International Capitalism. Through the National Revolution its people were purged of alien diseases and America became again American."

"Hail the Martyrdom in the Bijou Theater!" roar Shagpoke's youthful hearers when he is finished.

"Hail, Lemuel Pitkin!"

"All hail, the American Boy!"